Different Worlds
DIAMONDS
and
DENIM

Lisa Dane

BERKLEY BOOKS, NEW YORK

DIFFERENT WORLDS:
DIAMONDS AND DENIM

A Berkley Book / published by arrangement with
the author

PRINTING HISTORY
Berkley edition / June 1992

ISBN: 0-425-13300-1

A BERKLEY BOOK® TM 757,375
Berkley Books are published by The Berkley Publishing Group,
200 Madison Avenue, New York, New York 10016.
The name "BERKLEY" and the "B" logo
are trademarks belonging to Berkley Publishing Corporation.

PRINTED IN THE UNITED STATES OF AMERICA

10 9 8 7 6 5 4 3 2 1

Dear Reader,

Welcome to *DIFFERENT WORLDS!*

I hope you enjoy this brand-new romance series by the tremendously talented Lisa Dane. It's called *Different Worlds*, and it's all about the way love sometimes strikes the oddest of couples—and the way a relationship can be a compromise (and, sometimes, a comedy!). Some couples seem to have nothing in common . . . yet, there's a certain magical spark that draws them together—and *keeps* them together— no matter how maddeningly different their worlds. I think you'll treasure the special love stories in the *Different Worlds* collection—because their message is something we should never forget: *Love conquers all!*

Enjoy!

The Editor

To Adele Leone,
agent and troubleshooter

prologue

THE YOUNG MAN EASED AWAY FROM THE CHILD'S SIDE, careful not to disturb her much-needed rest. She had cried for her mother every night for two weeks, sometimes sobbing herself into hysterics, sometimes weeping quietly. His own sorrow was carefully kept inside—where it could gnaw at his soul.

Restlessly his eyes roamed over the stark features of the room. Her clothes were laid out, waiting for the morning when he would take her to the new school, adding fresh horrors to her narrow world. The posters on the wall were familiar, as was the cheap furniture. But the soft glow of the night-light was new. It created alternate pools of light and shadow on the threadbare carpet.

Did the night-light indeed keep the child safe from the invisible monsters that stalked her? It didn't keep them from haunting him. Tomorrow she would grieve over attending classes at a strange school while he chafed at the loss of his own education. Yet what other option had there been? To support the child he had to find a job. He could no longer afford the luxury of finishing his degree.

He stood at the foot of the bed staring at the now-drying paths the tears had left on the little girl's cheeks, at the way her bright carroty hair spread across the stark white of the pillowcase, at the desperate way she clutched the faded, well-loved stuffed dog to her chest. She was only six years old. So young to be left alone.

But she wasn't alone. She had him. And he was too young to have the care of this tiny, delicate being. His sister.

Quietly, he left the room, leaving the door open so that he could hear when she woke, hear if yet another nightmare threatened her.

He went into the tiny bathroom, splashed cold water on his face, stared at his reflection in the mirror. A few weeks ago he'd looked his twenty years. He'd been on the brink of beginning his own life. Now he was haggard. Lines of stress and sorrow were already working to make him look older. He ran a hand through his thick hair. His eyes burned with the effort to hold back his own grief. His jaw clenched tightly, its squared lines jutting with the effort.

Tomorrow his new existence would begin. He would become more than just a brother to the little girl. He would be father and mother as well, the breadwinner and caretaker of their now-dwindled family.

But tonight was still his alone. She was asleep. He envied her; sleep was an elusive goal for him. Nighttime was when he relived the scene on the freeway, saw once again the tangled bits of metal that had been his parents' car as it protruded from beneath the semi. They'd come west to visit him, to see what fascinated him so about Los

Angeles. What, they had asked, did it have that their quiet little midwestern town didn't?

He pushed the memory away. Far away, he hoped. The future was all that mattered now. His sister's future. He would don his father's gray suit in the morning and begin a career in banking. Stuck at a cashier's counter, his own future would be set. A future he loathed. But for Lyanne he would do it.

Weary, tense, his soul hurting, he slid the sash of the window open. Outside the view was of other dingy buildings. A far cry from the neat rows of brick houses back in Illinois. The one that had been his home was now up for sale. Silently he promised to move Lyanne to a better neighborhood once the house sold. For now his bachelor digs would have to suffice. He'd never thought of the flat as shabby before. It had been bohemian, suiting the life-style of a college student. The apartment was no home for a six-year-old girl, though. Of course, he could have picked up and left Los Angeles, could have put the city behind him and returned to the small town, lived in the house he'd grown up in. A home where he'd constantly see mental images of his mother and father, memories that would make the pain of their loss all the more poignant.

He leaned out the open window, breathing in the fumes of the city, the exhaust of cars, the pungent smells of the overflowing trash bin three stories below. He threw one leg over the sill and sat balanced on the window ledge. One foot drawn up on the sill, the other dangling far above the street, he leaned back. From this position he could catch a glimpse of open sky between the buildings. A piece of hazy gray firmament that could be studded with stars, for all he knew. How often did one see the stars in the city? Not often enough.

Lyanne deserved stars. Clean air, trees, grass . . . all the things he'd taken for granted growing up.

She'd lost her parents but he'd make sure she didn't lose anything else. He'd move her out of the city, out where the air was clean and the stars glistened in all their glory every night.

In the meantime, he'd view them in fantasy. For one final night he'd pursue his own dream of being a writer.

His eyes on the sliver of night sky, the man propped the notebook on his upraised knee. His pencil moved quickly over the page.

The twin moons rose in unison on the night of Kakert, painting the crags and valleys with a luminous blue-green-white light, revealing in harsh detail the cruel features of the planet Klakith.

one

THE TIP OF THE PENCIL SNAPPED.

"Wait a minute," Kristine Jackson growled into the phone receiver, and fumbled for a new pencil. The dozen goldenrod-yellow #2's in the jar on her desk resembled a bouquet of headless flowers. She sorted through them, pushing one after another aside, looking for a usable point. Frustrated, she dumped the container out, letting the rejects roll off onto the floor, until she found a semi-sharpened one. Kris scowled at it. The pencil was short and had rows of not-so-neat teeth marks where she'd chewed on it during a difficult session with now long-forgotten itineraries. The pencil's tip was worn down, but it would suffice.

"Okay, shoot," she said into the receiver.

"Roidan Ryder," the voice on the phone said, and spelled it for her.

Kris frowned. She recognized the name. The man was just a writer. Tame stuff for a woman who'd just coped with a heavy metal rock-and-roll band for three months.

"Listen, Halsey," Kris said, before the caller could continue. "I just got back. I really need time to recover from the tour. You can find somebody else to baby-sit this guy."

Joel Halsey wasn't an easy person to put off, though. "What? You want to vegetate? Krissy, baby doll! You lived through a hellish ninety days holding hands with that group . . . what's it called?"

"Dead Heat."

"Horrendous name." He paused. "Catchy, though."

Kris sighed and ran a hand through her wet hair. Its short cut made the damp blond strands stand up in spikes. "Halsey," she moaned. "I'm tired! If you think it's easy to keep four oversexed musicians in line, you're wrong. A kindergarten class from hell would have been a snap by comparison."

"Exactly why you should take this assignment," he insisted. "It's totally laid back, Krissy! You can recover in the mountains while you charm Ryder into promoting the movie."

Her eyes narrowed but Kris settled back in her high-backed chair. It was upholstered in a flame stitch of various shades of cream. The carpet in her study was the tone of coffee with a generous dollop of milk, as were the curtains and the satin-finish wallpaper. A single large painting added a dash of color to the room—it was a swath of pink across an otherwise eggshell canvas. Her mother had decorated the place for her the year before while Kris was bird-dogging a soap-opera queen through a cologne promotion tour. Belinda Jackson went through phases, and this had been what she called her subtle period.

It suited Kris, though. She was rarely at home and it was pleasant to have her apartment look nothing like the many hotel and motel rooms in which she spent her time while on tour.

She gazed absently at the angle of the slats on the venetian blinds. If she squinted hard she could fancy being able to see the still-bare branches of trees in Central Park. If she only had the courage to hang up on Halsey, she could open the blinds, stand at the window and enjoy her high-priced view of the park.

Since she didn't have the guts to slam the phone down, Kris stretched her long legs out, digging her bare toes into the thick café au lait carpet.

Halsey's call had caught her in the shower. There were still droplets of water clinging to her skin. They sparkled in the light from the lamp on the desk. Kris used the hem of her ivory terry-cloth robe to pat herself dry. If she'd ignored the ringing, she'd still be reveling in the marvelous feel of steaming hot water against her tense shoulders. But habit was hard to break. For too long she'd made mad dashes to the phone. Five years ago she'd been waiting for modeling assignments, but more recently Kris's career had taken an abrupt change. For the better, she admitted. With Joel Halsey's help she'd entered the world of public relations and promotion. With his guidance she'd learned to be the essence of sanity on the promotion tours of celebrities. Traveling with composers, conductors, musicians, actors and actresses, ex-politicians, and authors, Kris had been the person who got them to meetings, countered unhealthy press, protected the celeb from the fans (or, in the case of Dead Heat, the more innocent fans from the celebs). She worked out the itineraries, blocked all attempts (if possible) of her clients to deviate from the planned schedules. She handled emergencies, comforted, petted, and, in truth, baby-sat the flighty egomaniacs with whom she worked. Fortunately, the celebrities were never her employers. She worked for manufacturers, studios, recording companies, and publishers.

It was exciting, but it meant she was rarely able to enjoy the comfort of her New York City apartment. She was always on the go, hitting one town after another, checking airline schedules against interview or performance schedules, heading off determined fans, cajoling determined celebrities. She loved every minute of it.

Joel Halsey made sure that she was paid very well for every minute of her time. She didn't really have to work. She'd been fairly successful as a leggy model of sportswear and swimsuits, and had a very generous trust fund from her father's estate. Kris was able to afford every luxury she'd ever wanted.

Now she wanted some time to enjoy those luxuries. All she had to do was say no.

After other tours, Halsey had understood her need to have time to herself. Sometimes she'd spend a couple weeks with her sister Sandra. Other times it would be a blissful month on a fairly deserted beach. She'd been toying with the idea of a cruise. The vacations were invigorating because, in the end, she always became bored with leisure and returned to New York eager for a new assignment. But, for some reason, this time Halsey had no intention of letting Kris recuperate first.

"Baby doll," he cooed, his voice fairly dripping with syrup. "Roidan Ryder is a pussycat compared to Dead Heat. The man is a veritable hermit. Lives up in the mountains and turns out two sci-fi fantasy novels a year. Like clockwork. Asteroid Books loves him! Not only does the public clamor for his stuff, the man never misses a deadline!"

Kris drew saintly halos over every letter in Roidan Ryder's name on her notepad. "If he's such a paragon, why do they need me?"

Halsey cleared his throat. "I mentioned he was a hermit, didn't I?"

"Lives in a cave?"

"For all we know. No one's ever met him. He's yet to sign his first autograph. His editor has never seen him, just talks to him on the phone."

"A cave with a phone," Kris mumbled, and colored in the *O* and *D* of the writer's name to look like the crossed eyes of a cartoon character.

"They would leave him alone except for the movie," Halsey explained.

"What movie?"

"*Klakith*. Loosely based on his first book, *The Dealer of Klakith*."

At her silence, Halsey's voice dropped to a chiding whine. "Surely, you've read some of the chronicles of Klakith," he said. "Ryder's working on the twentieth volume right now."

"You don't usually leave me much time for recreational reading," Kris pointed out testily. She didn't mention that her taste didn't run to science-fiction stories.

"Okay, so I'll fill you in. He's got this macho hero named Dalwulf who lives on the planet Klakith. It's a pretty progressive place in some ways, backward in others. To promote world peace, the women of one land mass are traded to the men of another. That way they mix the races up nicely and are one big happy family."

Kris glared at Ryder's name on her notepad. "You want me to go pander to a chauvinist, is that it?"

"Right!"

She ground her teeth. Audibly. The sound didn't slow Halsey down a bit.

"All you have to do is convince Ryder that he'll make a lot more loot if he goes—and I hasten to stress this for your benefit as well, Krissy—on a *very* short, very select tour to promote the movie. And the books, of course. I don't think any of the Klakith stories are out of print. He'll make a second bloody fortune with a minimum of energy expended."

Kris took a deep, calming breath. "Halsey . . ."

"Baby doll," he pleaded. "If you love me, you'll at least talk to the studio and publisher about it."

"Halsey . . ."

"Great," he said. "My office. Tomorrow morning. Eleven. I'll take you to Le Bernardin for lunch afterward." He hung up before she could refuse.

Belinda Jackson surveyed her glass of white wine with a scrutiny that made her daughter feel she was looking for grape seeds.

"You know what you need?" Belinda inquired.

Kris leaned forward, her elbows on the glass-topped table, her own Waterford goblet balanced between her hands. The dining area was another of Belinda's flings into interior decorating. This time the color scheme was salmon. The circular dining table was complemented by a sideboard, also glass topped. The four dining chairs were straight-backed, armless, and covered in a blushing salmon watered-silk fabric that matched the wall covering. A tangled mass of welded metal graced one wall pretending to be birds in flight. Or a lily pond. Kris had never really decided which.

She surveyed her mother across the remains of dinner. Since neither of the women had developed culinary talents, and Kris was tired of restaurant food, they'd stayed in for their reunion, sustaining themselves with a large salad.

"I know what you're going to tell me *you* think I need," Kris said.

Belinda smiled slightly. She was careful never to give a full smile and deepen the finely etched lines around her mouth. Her blond hair was a paler shade than it had been when Kris had left on tour with Dead Heat. Apparently Belinda had done more at the exclusive health spa than merely lose fifteen pounds. Kris had to admit that her mother looked fantastic, though. And the way that her casual designer-label sweater and slacks clung to her rehabilitated figure insured that Belinda would be bragging about a new escort the next time she visited her daughter.

"What you need," Belinda said, "is a man in your life."

Kris gave a ladylike snort. "I just had four men in my life," she reminded.

"Oh, no, darling. You can hardly call the members of Dead Heat men. I'm sure they were, but I don't fancy a man who wears leather and has hair down to his rear end as a son-in-law."

Same old song, Kris thought. "I don't want to get married," she reminded her mother.

Belinda's lips contorted to express disappointment. "I've been a bad example to you, haven't I?"

"Not at all," Kris soothed. She'd stopped counting the number of marriages and engagements her mother had contracted. Her older sister Sandra hadn't felt the strain quite the same. Perhaps that had been because she'd spent more time with her own father and his second wife, a woman who was a much more stable emotional force than their flighty mother. Kris's father had been a very successful stockbroker whose heart hadn't been as sound as his portfolio. She'd kept his name, but her memory of him was very faint. The fact that between husbands Belinda reverted to the surname of Jackson as well had always seemed a bit romantic to Kris. As if Thurman Jackson still held a part of her mother's heart.

"I don't want to get married," Kris repeated. "I like my life, my job. I like traveling. I like the excitement. I . . ."

"Selfish child," Belinda interrupted. "Think of me, darling. Don't you want me to have the pleasure of bouncing your little ones on my knee?"

"Grandchildren? Mother," Kris murmured in amusement. "You're too young to be a grandmother. You've told me so each time Sandra gives birth." Her sister now had three darling children.

Belinda waved the facts away. "Kristine. I want to talk about you."

"Me." Kris was far from enthusiastic.

"I met the most perfect man for you, darling," Belinda insisted. "A heart specialist. He is very well respected. Quite handsome. I've invited him to dinner Friday night to meet you."

Inwardly, Kris groaned. Her mother's idea of the perfect mate and hers differed . . . drastically. Belinda kept producing men of wealth and position, men who were respected by the community, men who were window-dressing perfect. Kris always suspected them. She'd seen too many of their kind breeze through her mother's life. That outward panache always disguised something disreputable. Insider trading, faulty business ethics, personality problems, alcoholism, drugs, women—Kris had seen them all. As a result, none of her mother's conquests had been the sort of man with whom Kris wished to spend a lifetime. If she ever changed her mind about marriage, Kris wanted it to last forever.

"Friday? Oh, Mother," she moaned. "If only you'd asked me first."

Belinda wasn't in the least fooled by the theatrical tone her daughter chose. Kristine had been weaseling out of introductions for a number of years.

"Don't try to tell me you have plans already," Belinda said complacently. "I know you always take a couple weeks off between assignments. You haven't been in town long enough to have other engagements yet. So I'll expect you at eight."

Kris took a quick sip of wine. The bouquet was lost on her, though. She was trying to find a way out of meeting the heart specialist.

"You're right," she said carefully. "I usually do have time off. But not this time. Halsey's already booked me for another tour."

Belinda's lovely eyes narrowed in suspicion. "So soon? What is it this time?" Her voice became quite sarcastic. "Another group of rock and rollers? A concert pianist? An aging actress selling beauty secrets?"

Kris had never accepted any assignment without learning as many personal details as she could about the celebrity with whom she would be traveling. She liked knowing the public person, but more specifically, she wanted to learn the quirks of the private person. It made it easier on both of them when she did the scheduling to know their likes and dislikes. This time, however, Kris took the leap blindfolded.

"I can't be there, Mother," she said. "You see, on Friday I'll be in the mountains with Roidan Ryder."

two

WHEN HALSEY HAD SAID THAT ROIDAN RYDER LIVED in the mountains, Kris had thought he meant somewhere in nearby Vermont or maybe as far away as Colorado. She'd never envisioned the wilds of southern Utah as her destination.

She'd flown into Las Vegas on Thursday and soaked up one final evening of civilization before confronting the hermit in his cave. Halsey'd made reservations for her at Klakith Lodge outside of Cedar City in Utah. But to get there she had to drive up a series of icy switchback roads.

Back in New York the landscape had been stretching, rousing itself in the first weeks of spring. But here in the mountains, Mother Earth was still slumbering beneath a shroud of snow. Tall pine trees rose on both sides of the narrow road. Signs warning of deer and falling rock did nothing to improve Kris's mood. There was little traffic ahead of her—or passing her inbound for the town she'd reluctantly left at the foot of the mountain. Cedar City was no more than a village, as far as Kris was concerned. It was pretty, if you liked hamlets. It boasted a college that held a celebrated summer-long Shakespeare Festival. But right now summer was only a dream in this cold, icy world.

Kris took a final curve around the mountain and, from the corner of her eye, spotted the rustic signpost for Klakith Lodge. She turned the rented silver BMW onto the narrow rutted track. The suspension system underwent rigorous testing, bouncing along the snowy path. A couple of times the car slid dangerously close to the shoulder, but Kris persevered, swinging the wheel in the direction the BMW chose rather than the one she wanted. She managed to stay out of the ditches on either side, but the sudden appearance of a stretch of heavy metal chain blocking the end of the lane defeated her. Slamming down the brake, Kris felt the vehicle hesitate, then slide as it hit another slick bit of ice. She hit the chain at five miles per hour. The barrier held. But so did the combination of ice, snow, and mud. Its tires spinning in place, the BMW refused to go either backwards or forwards.

Kris sat fuming, her fingers in their chamois-leather driving gloves drumming impatiently on the steering wheel. She hadn't wanted this assignment. The chain showed that the hermit didn't relish her visit either. He knew she was coming. Halsey himself had assured her that he'd rung Ryder's cave a number of times, making reservations, getting directions, wheedling unsuccessfully for someone to pick Kris up at the airport. With the Brianhead ski resort so close to Cedar City, they had both expected that the lodge Ryder owned would be opened. Ryder didn't care for snow skiing, they'd been told. He preferred the peace offered by fishing.

Klakith Lodge was located in the Dixie National Forest on the edge of a mountain lake. Kris could see the sun shining on the melted surface from where she sat stranded. If the lake was nearby, that meant that the lodge itself was close. She pulled open the car door and stepped out. Her high-heeled boots sank into the mud.

A fearless cardinal fluttered down from the surrounding trees to perch on the metal chain. The bird eyed her with interest. Kris was sure she could discern amusement in its eyes. Bright red feathers ruffled as it resettled, inching to a more comfortable link. High above, a short raucous call sounded. The bird looked up as another, less brilliantly colored flash of feather fluttered from one branch to another. Finding the lady bird more to his liking, the cardinal forgot Kris and took off after his mate.

"Fine, desert me," Kris muttered. She slammed the door of the BMW closed and sloshed her way around the barrier and on down the track toward the lake.

The lodge was visible as soon as she cleared the trees. It wasn't large. It wasn't the A-framed building she'd half expected. Nor was it a fanciful version of a Swiss chalet. Kris stopped and stood still, staring in disbelief. It was better than a cave, of course, but still . . . a log cabin? Not just one either, but a series of smaller cabins grouped around a larger one. Any moment one of those doors would open and Daniel Boone would step out, blunderbuss, powder horn, fringed leggings, and all.

The green branches and mastlike trunks of mountain pine framed the main lodge. Smoke curled in a picturesque, lazy movement from the chimney of the two-story building. Dormers pushed from the neatly shingled roof. A long porch ran the length of the overgrown wilderness cabin, housing a rustic bench and a large pile of chopped wood.

There were only two things that jarred the setting firmly back into the late twentieth century. Instead of a horse and sleigh, a dark blue Isuzu Trooper was parked before the hitching rail. And from somewhere close by, the sound of Steve Winwood blasted the peace of the day.

Figuring rock music meant civilization, Kris followed the sound down to the lake. Her boots collected more mud. Her toes began to feel the bite of the cold as the soft leather soaked up the dampness. There was a slight breeze coming off the lake. It whipped her cheeks to a bright red, attacked the carefully styled sweep of her short blond hair. It made her blue eyes tear. The lake seemed to shimmer with an unearthly light when viewed through a watery haze.

Kris zeroed in on the sound of Winwood's guitar. It led her to a small dock. Made of rough, weathered wooden boards and sturdy metal pilings, it jutted out into the lake about thirty feet. At the end a man leaned back in a plastic lawn chair, right foot balanced on a tackle box. A heavy plaid blanket was draped over the outstretched leg. An Irish setter lay on top of his left foot. The dog looked up at Kris's approach but didn't growl, snarl, or even get up to investigate. The man didn't question her presence either. He continued to stare out over the lake, over the end of the fishing pole, at the undisturbed red and white bobber that danced on the surface of the water.

Kris stormed up to him, her footsteps ringing on the wooden walk, her boots leaving clumps of mud in a Hansel-and-Gretel type trail behind her. "Hey you!" she shouted over the music. "Sport! Is this Klakith Lodge?"

The man didn't turn. He just nodded. Kris wasn't sure if he was answering her question or had merely fallen asleep.

"I'm looking for Roidan Ryder," she continued.

The man dropped a gloved hand on the dog's head and scratched. The setter's tongue lolled out in sheer pleasure. "Not many folks come here looking for Ryder," the man said. His eyes never left the bobbing end of his line in the water.

Kris stormed closer, moving so that the insolent male would be forced to look her in the eye. "Listen, I'm not some autograph seeker, buster. I'm expected."

The fisherman looked up then. Kris was sure she'd somehow stumbled into the Twilight Zone. Surely she had landed on the planet Klakith, and Dalwulf, dealer in female pulchritude, was sizing up her market qualities.

After committing herself to the Ryder project, Kris had stopped at the nearest bookstore and bought a few of the Klakith novels. She'd read through the first two so far. But even with that brief view of Ryder's fantasy world, Kris could recognize his protagonist, Dalwulf the Dealer.

The man on the dock had the same thick shock of reddish-brown hair, the same sun-warmed complexion, the same unruly brows, long patrician nose, and golden feral eyes. His jaw was squared, his lips unsmiling. Dressed in a heavy fisherman's sweater, topped with an olive-drab coat, he looked the equivalent of a hunched linebacker.

He didn't get up. He continued to stare at her. A bit malevolently.

"Are you Ryder?" Kris asked loudly, still trying to be heard over the music.

He leaned over and shut off the portable tape player. In the silence Kris could hear the water lap gently at the dock pilings.

Still seated, the man sized her up one more time, from her short cap of blond hair on down over her long black marten coat to the tips of her muddy boots. "Do I look like Ryder?" he asked at last.

Kris had no intention of telling him whom she thought he looked like. The oaf would probably take it as a compliment if she said he resembled the barbarian in Ryder's books. She turned the collar of her coat higher, as if protecting herself from a chill rather than the speculative look in his golden eyes. "No one knows what Ryder looks like," she declared. "Which you obviously already know, Mr. . . . ?"

He smiled maliciously at her unsubtle suggestion that he introduce himself. "You must be Kristine Jackson," he said. "I was told to expect you."

"But not to welcome me, I suppose. That's why the road was still blocked by a chain."

His grin widened. "You took the old road. Didn't you read the sign? We haven't used that route in years." He turned his attention to the dog, pulling its ears. The animal drooled in pleasure. "I suppose we'll have to call a tow truck for your car."

His calm acceptance and unconcern rubbed Kris the wrong way. "Today, I hope," she growled. "Before then, I hope someone"— she stared hard at him —"will retrieve my luggage and show me to my suite."

"A suite," he mused.

Kris stood her ground. "That is the accommodation that was reserved in my name." Her eyes narrowed in suspicion. "It is ready, isn't it?"

"Lady, you can have more than a suite as far as I'm concerned. You can have a whole cabin to yourself."

She looked back at the tiny log buildings. "A cabin?" she repeated faintly. God only knew what it would be like in one of those rustic shacks. They looked like they'd been thrown together in frontier days and forgotten. "I wouldn't want to put the staff to additional work," Kris hastened to assure the man. "Rooms at the main lodge will be sufficient, Mr. . . . er . . ."

This time he condescended to fill in the gap. "Cheney. Adam Cheney. I manage the lodge."

Kris looked at the fishing pole, at the line that trailed into the water.

"It's the off season," Adam said, his voice still amused at her attitude.

"If you say so. Now if you'll just . . ."

He had already turned his attention back to his fishing. "Go on up to the main cabin." He threw the words over his shoulder in an afterthought. "Lyanne will see to your comfort."

Kris wasn't moving. "And who is Lyanne?"

Adam's lips twitched. He settled more comfortably in his chair. "My assistant," he said.

The oaf! Kris stormed off toward the larger of the log buildings. Adam Cheney was worse than a barbarian. Dalwulf of Klakith probably had more manners. The Dealer would have stood up, would have been eager to help her. But Cheney . . .

Behind her Steve Winwood resumed his guitar lick, the sound echoing out over the water.

It wasn't Winwood but the cranked-up sounds of Def Leppard that blasted Kris at the main lodge. The song was a couple of years old, but that didn't diminish the enthusiasm with which the slender redhead belted out her own version, pleading to have someone "Pour Some Sugar" on her. She swiped at the mantel with a rainbow-colored feather duster as she sang, her hips twitching to the rhythm.

The girl was attractive enough to be window dressing in a rock music video. She had that same slinky look that the heavy metal bands favored. Despite the cold, damp temperatures outside, the young woman wore a very short, very tight denim skirt. Her body-hugging white blouse clung precariously to the tips of her shoulders and dipped sharply toward the valley between her breasts leaving the girl prey to the dangers of a severe chest cold. White cotton socks covered her feet and allowed her to skate a bit on the highly polished wood flooring as she danced. With her lush red hair falling in spiral curls halfway down her back, and vast expanses of bare skin showing, there was only one word Kris could think of that accurately described Adam Cheney's "assistant." *Bimbo*.

While she waited for a break in the music, Kris slid out of her coat and draped it over her arm. Although the outside of the lodge hadn't promised much in the way of comfort, the interior was a pleasant surprise. The stone fireplace was enormous and had been well constructed. Heat radiated from the fire that burned in the grate making the room toasty. Rustic benches formed a U-shaped seating area adjacent to the hearth arranged on an equally rustic braided area rug. Pillows in deep burgundy and forest green were plumped along the back of the settees. One wall was floor-to-ceiling built-in shelves that held an elaborate stereo system, magazines, and well-thumbed copies of the Klakith stories in both hardcover and paperback. A couple of armchairs, upholstered in deep brown leather, seemed very masculine compared to the country theme of the other furnishings. What surprised Kris was the lack of stuffed trophies of deer or elk on the walls.

At long last the song ground to a halt. The young woman with the feather duster put a spin on her own finale and spotted Kris waiting patiently just inside the door.

"Oh!" she squeaked. Then, just as Adam Cheney had done earlier, the girl gave Kris a quick head-to-toe inspection.

Kris wondered if her high-necked, powder-blue angora sweater would meet with approval or be considered too concealing by the nymph. Would the acid-washed jeans she'd thought appropriate for the mountains appear condescending? Or perhaps her full-length fur coat would instill a gleam of avarice in the young woman's eyes.

It was her thigh-high boots, however, that held her hostess's attention. They hugged Kris's legs and reached nearly to her hips.

"Wow!" the girl breathed in awe. "Where did you get those bitchin' boots?"

As a welcome, it was little better than Adam Cheney's growl had been. "Italy," Kris said, and stepped forward into the room. "Are you Lyanne?"

The girl nodded. The stiffened plume of her moussed bangs waved. She danced over to the stereo system and switched the sound down before answering. "Yep. You must be Ms. Jackson. Adam said you were coming," she said and beamed over her shoulder at Kris.

The place was run by incompetents. How did Roidan Ryder put up with Cheney and his little sugar? Obviously the writer had little to do with them, Kris decided. He probably just stayed away, safe in his sane little cave. Now if she could just get someone to point her toward his hole in the rock, she would dazzle Ryder with logic and drag him back into the civilized world.

Lyanne's head was cocked to one side. Her forehead was puckered in thought. "You look familiar," she said.

Kris tried to guess her hostess's age. That lush womanly body was deceptive. The creamy softness of the young woman's fresh, scrubbed face was equally confusing. She lived in the mountains, apparently alone with Adam Cheney. Could Lyanne be twenty-one? If she was, then she might remember Kris's career as a model. Would an airhead like this have bought *Vogue* and *Harper's Bazaar*, though?

"I've got it!" Lyanne shouted and made a mad dash further down the wall toward another section of the shelving. Her socks slid on the floor but Lyanne merely let the momentum carry her forward to her destination. Like a kid would.

Kris frowned. Definitely not one of *Vogue*'s subscribers. Then where . . . ?

Lyanne scrambled through a stack of magazines. Kris saw copies of *Seventeen*, *Tiger Beat*, and various movie magazines tossed temporarily aside before the girl found the star-studded cover of the issue she wanted. She turned pages quickly. "Here it is!" Lyanne looked up, her eyes shining. They were a golden color. Not as deeply dramatic in shade as Adam Cheney's but still rather startlingly attractive.

Reluctant, Kris draped her coat over the back of one of the settees and moved over to where Lyanne stood, magazines littering the floor at her feet.

The picture had been taken at the New Year's Eve concert in Los Angeles. She had dressed to blend with the crowd that night, Kris remembered . . . an insanity she had never repeated again during the Dead Heat tour. Her short, slim, ebony leather skirt had merely accented the shapely length of her black-stockinged legs. The matching bolero had offered glimpses of a low-cut, sequin-covered camisole. Rather than have her blond hair arranged in its usual smooth sweep, she'd played with the stubby locks till they had stood out in stagy, shaped spikes. If nothing else, the overall campy affect had kept the four members of Dead Heat drooling at her heels that evening rather than chasing down underage groupies. She hadn't realized one of the paparazzi had snapped a shot of her with the band, though. A rather compromising photograph at that.

"That's you, isn't it?" Lyanne demanded eagerly, her face alight with hero worship as she stabbed a finger at the picture in the magazine.

Kris sighed. "Yes, that's me," she admitted. The shot showed a leggy blond crushed to the bare chest of Dead Heat's lead singer, his hand spread suggestively on her rear end. *Former top fashion model Kristine, one of the intimates on Dead Heat's current tour, congratulates Tasker Fane on a successful performance*, the caption read. Too bad the photographer hadn't added a second shot, the one that would show Fane hobbling away, swearing the blow from her knee had ruined his career. Fearing permanent falsetto voices, none of the four musicians had tried to maul her during the rest of the tour.

"You know Tasker Fane!" Lyanne closed her eyes in ecstasy. "Wait till Becky hears about this. She is absolutely *in love* with Tasker Fane."

Her hostess was definitely not twenty-one, Kris decided. Instead, it looked like Adam Cheney had feathered his little love nest with very ripe jailbait. Did Roidan Ryder know? Kris thought again about how much the manager of Klakith Lodge resembled the hero of Ryder's fantasy tales. Lord, for all she knew, Lyanne might be part of the latest episode. Teenage airhead joins Dalwulf the Dealer's stock of marketable tail.

"Before you tell Becky the good news," Kris suggested, interrupting her young hostess's reveries, "do you think you could show me my room? And perhaps get Mr. Cheney or someone to bring my bags up? My car is—"

The main door slammed. In the entranceway a young man with long, shaggy, nutmeg-brown hair stood peeling off a bright blue ski jacket. He slung it over the pegs of the coatrack mounted on the wall behind the door. "Hey, Lye," he shouted without looking around. "There's a Beemer stuck on the old track! Does the big man know about it?"

The newcomer wore a black T-shirt with the Jack Daniel's logo prominently displayed across his chest. Or perhaps it was just the way the fabric stretched, accentuating the development of his pectoral muscles that made the advertisement stand out. His worn jeans were as close-fitting as a second skin. A baseball cap, worn backwards, kept his hair out of his face.

He turned and came to an abrupt halt, both in movement and speech, when he noticed Kris.

Lyanne was wide-eyed. "A Beemer? Oh, wow!"

Kris couldn't remember ever being impressed by a car. But Lyanne was enthusiastic about nearly everything, it seemed.

"I'm absolute bonkers, Dean," the girl told the young man. She rushed across the room, magazine in hand. "Look," she urged him. "This is Ms. Jackson. It's her BMW. She's a famous model *and* she knows Tasker Fane of Dead Heat."

Dean looked suitably impressed.

"She's here," Lyanne continued in a rush of enthusiasm, "to get Roidan Ryder to promote that movie they made."

Dean burst into laughter. Lyanne joined in, hers a higher-pitched giggle. "Good luck," Dean said.

She was used to reluctant celebrities, Kris reminded herself. Even Tasker Fane hadn't wanted her sticking a finger in his pie. But she'd never run into such a negative reaction among a celebrity's entourage before. Although she didn't understand what position Dean held at the lodge, it was fairly clear that he ran tame about the place.

"Thank you," Kris murmured dryly. Just what she needed. A lack of confidence in her ability. Well, she'd show them. The skeptical Dean, the airheaded Lyanne, and the infuriatingly amused Adam Cheney. "Could someone bring my luggage up from the car?" Kris smiled brightly at Lyanne, giving her the wide grin for which she'd once been famous. "Perhaps Mr. Cheney could be motivated to free my car?" she wheedled softly. If anyone could twist the taciturn man around her finger it was obviously the slinky redhead.

It wasn't Lyanne who answered, though. The young man named Dean grunted and reached for his jacket again. "I'll see to both," he said, and let the door slam closed behind him.

Lyanne didn't seem affected by the blast of cold air from outside. She hugged the movie magazine to her chest, her foolish grin wider than ever. "Dean will see to everything," she assured Kris.

Slightly irritated that the ogre down on the dock wouldn't be dragged away from his fishing, Kris tried again. "What about Mr. Cheney?" she demanded.

"Adam?" Lyanne asked in surprise. "Oh, he doesn't mind Dean helping. Anyway, Adam's pretty useless for things like that."

Useless for menial tasks such as carrying luggage and freeing mired automobiles, huh. What actually was Adam Cheney good at, then?

Lyanne twinkled brightly, the magazine covering the scoop of her low-cut neckline.

Then again, Kris thought, maybe she didn't really want to know exactly what Adam Cheney's talents were, after all.

three

THAT DAY ADAM'S TALENTS DID NOT INCLUDE FISHING.

He stared listlessly at the bobber as it rode the gentle lap of the lake. He didn't really expect the trout to be stupid enough to be tempted by a lone marshmallow on a hook. Anyway, Lyanne considered an out-of-season guest a reason to celebrate with steak for dinner, so even if one of the fish was suicidal, it would just have ended up in the freezer. It took some of the pleasure out of fishing to just store the catch away.

Adam sighed. At his feet, the Irish setter shifted position and sighed as well.

"Just as sick of this as I am, are you, pooch?" He rubbed the setter's head. The dog's feathered tail beat happily against the dock.

"What did you think of our visitor?" Adam asked. "A bit bitchy?"

The dog murmured as if answering.

"I beg your pardon, sweetheart. Don't want to be classed with her, do you? Feisty, then. Cocksure. You know the type."

The setter rolled her eyes.

"Yeah," Adam agreed lazily. "I noticed the resemblance. She looks too damn much like Emling. That cropped ice-blond hair, those big lake-blue eyes. We don't know what she looks like under those pelts, though."

The dog put her chin on his knee, resting against his good leg.

"My guess is that she'll look much too good," Adam said. "Her skin might not have that alluring blue cast that Dalwulf finds so fascinating in the Normass women. But then, I'm not Dalwulf."

The setter made a derogatory sound in her throat.

"Well, I'm not," Adam insisted. "It was a foul day when I wrote his description, you know. Lyanne's first day at school in Los Angeles. I wanted to feel capable of slaying all her dragons, so I created a hero who didn't have my failings."

The patient dog had heard it all before and indicated as such to her master.

Adam's gaze turned toward the lodge. A warm glow lit the windows. "Lord. What am I going to do with her?"

"Woolf," his companion suggested.

"No, not Emling. Or the she-devil either. What am I going to do with Lyanne?"

The dog turned her muzzle toward the log building as well, her eyes appearing as concerned as his.

"She's sixteen years old," Adam murmured. "Where did the time go?"

Hadn't it only been yesterday that he'd watched the paramedics pull Lyanne unscathed from the back seat of their parents' crushed sedan? The family had only arrived from Illinois two days before. His mother, Anne, had tried to hide the fact that she found his tiny apartment appalling. His father, Lyle, had been quietly amused at her reaction and more interested in how Adam's studies were progressing. Lyanne, the darling late addition to the family, had only wanted to know when they were going to Disneyland.

Adam hoped the family had had a lovely day at the park. It had been his parents' last.

Those first two years without them had been sheer hell. He wanted to give his sister so much, but finances had been slim. The neat brick house back in Illinois had taken forever to sell. In the end, he'd accepted an offer far below market value just to get out from under the responsibility. His job at the bank had felt stifling, but at least he had his weekends and evenings free to spend with Lyanne.

The friends he'd been so close to at UCLA had dropped away, unable or unwilling to accept that Adam was no longer free to indulge in parties that lasted until dawn. Nothing in his life was spontaneous now. It all had to be planned around his tight budget and the ability to find a baby-sitter for his young sister. Dates had been few. Young single women just weren't attracted to the idea of a ready-made family. They preferred careers and an excitement he couldn't offer.

Although he was not Lyanne's father, he was most definitely a single parent, filling a paternal rather than a brotherly role in her life. Even when he began attending PTA meetings, the single mothers he met were more interested in complaining about ex-husbands to each other than in a romance with a much younger man who was tied down himself. So he'd stopped looking for an enduring relationship, had withdrawn to the narrow world that revolved around his little sister.

It had been to combat the continued frustration with his job and social life that each evening he'd pursued his dream of being a writer. The adventures of Dalwulf the Dealer were his outlet, his escape.

He'd been unsure of himself, unsure of the story's reception at any publisher. It had taken all of his courage to mail it off, hiding himself from ridicule by inventing the persona of Roidan Ryder. When the editor at Asteroid Books had called, he'd clung to the fiction that Ryder preferred to act through an agent. An agent named Adam Cheney.

That had been nearly ten years ago.

Now they wanted him to go public, to confess to a dual identity none of them even suspected. Now, of all times, when he could no longer handle Lyanne.

She'd been such a model child for years. Never any trouble at school, never throwing tantrums. Polite, bright, pretty. That had been Lyanne.

Adam hardly recognized the teenager who had blossomed to womanhood early. Boys had flocked to his door. He could deal with them. It was the young men from the college that were harder to oust. Dean Taggart, in particular.

Adam heard Taggart's ancient truck rumble along the main entrance road—the paved one that the dragon lady from New York had missed by a hundred feet. Dean parked his rusty vehicle next to Adam's new Trooper, waved a greeting, and barreled through the front door of the lodge without knocking.

Adam and the dog sighed in unison, their breath filling the cold air with visible clouds of condensation. "That's what comes from living in a public building," Adam told the setter. "You get visitors who make themselves at home whether you want them to or not."

It was difficult to admit Dean Taggart had been more of a help than a hindrance since the Thanksgiving holidays, especially for a man who'd become so self-sufficient over the years. When Taggart emerged within minutes from the house, Adam was pleased to see the young man was making a beeline for the old rutted road.

What was it about Taggart that he didn't like? Was it the unkempt look? The kid fancied himself a guitarist and dressed the part of a seedy rock-and-roll musician. Still, Dean pitched in on chores at the lodge without being asked. And without being paid.

Adam hoped his young sister wasn't paying for the brawn with any services of her own. He watched her carefully, but despite her curvaceous woman's body and tight clothes, Lyanne didn't seem to have entered any new phase of grown-up knowledge. She was still a child in so many ways—which was just the way he wanted her to stay. There was no hurry for her to grow up. Not like there had been for him.

Dean Taggart wasn't a child, though. He'd spent four years in the Air Force after graduating from the local high school. He'd returned last fall just before the holidays. And he'd been a fixture at Klakith Lodge since then.

Lyanne's best friend Becky's mother had told him not to worry, that the more he tried to interfere with his sister's first romance, the more inclined she would be to believe it was the great love of her life and do something stupid. Adam didn't want that. He only wanted the best in life for Lyanne. The scruffy son of a hardware salesman didn't fit that mold.

"I'm a snob to find fault with Dean's background, aren't I?" Adam asked the dog. Of late, the setter was the only being available to listen to him. The hound wasn't much of a conversationalist, she often let him know that she disagreed with his opinion, and she never offered viable solutions to his problems, be they personal or fictional. But she was always there . . . something that could not be said for his suddenly mobile sister.

"It's the age difference, I suppose. Dean's age. Lye's age. And the circumstances," Adam said. "I don't want her to grow up. And until she got her driver's license, I was doing a pretty good job of sheltering her from the outside world. But now . . ."

The setter didn't think much of his fretting. She yawned.

"If only it weren't for this damn leg," Adam insisted and shifted uneasily in his chair. The stiffly held weight of his right leg itched. As usual. He'd been outside long enough for the cold to penetrate the many layers of wool Lyanne had wrapped around him earlier. "It makes me antsy."

The dog whined shortly, as if reminding him that only a few days remained till his next visit to the doctor in town. An appointment he'd been looking forward to for four long months now.

"Easy for you to say," Adam chided. "It won't be the same, you know. The damage is already done, not just to the leg, but to my life. Lyanne's found her wings."

The setter tilted her head, watching a set of fluttering wings come to perch on one of the dock pilings. A second flash of feathers joined it.

Adam stared at the two birds quietly. They eyed him in interested silence, then fluffed their bodies till the feathers looked fuller, more brilliant. Ignoring the man and his dog, the more brightly colored male began grooming his mate.

"Hell," Adam grumbled. "As if I don't have enough to worry about. Lyanne's bound to decide she's in love now! It's spring!"

* * *

Up at the main lodge, Lyanne came down the stairs from the second floor, her hurried footsteps sounding more like a herd of charging elephants than one slim teenager. She had pulled on a shocking-pink turtleneck sweater, fleece-lined boots, and a cotton-candy-colored ski jacket. Her pink earmuffs clashed a bit with her copper hair. The girl's smile was still as bright and happy as a child's. It was disconcerting to see such trust and pleasure.

"Adam said to give you the closest cabin. It isn't the newest, but he didn't think you'd care to be very far away from the main lodge," Lyanne babbled, pulling the front door open.

Kris followed her hostess back into the cold, damp, dismally clouded day. She huddled in the warmth of her fur, hiding her nose in its soft, thick nap.

Lyanne bounded off the porch. Kris followed at a more sedate rate. The melting snow curled up around the toes of her boots, resoaking them. A suite, she prayed. Let the inside of this building be as warm and surprisingly livable as the lodge.

The gods of Klakith didn't grant Kris's wish. As the door swung open, she wondered if she was being tested.

"Oh, drat," Lyanne said. "I forgot to restock the stove."

Drat didn't cover it as far as Kris was concerned. Her own thoughts hovered closer to blasphemy. The cabin was nearly as cold inside as outside. Her lips tightly drawn, Kris quietly consigned Joel Halsey, Roidan Ryder, and Adam Cheney, in particular, to Beelzebub's keeping.

Lyanne wasted no time, using a convenient towel to open the metal door of the Franklin stove. In nothing flat she had hefted cut-to-size logs and kindling into the hungry mouth and turned it into a blazing inferno. The heat was welcome but didn't radiate much farther than a foot from the stove.

"It will take a little while to warm the cabin up," Lyanne explained.

An understatement as far as Kris was concerned. She buried her hands deeper in the pockets of her coat.

Undaunted, Lyanne blithely guided Kris through the rest of her "suite."

The Hilton doesn't have to worry, Kris reflected silently. There was the central room with the Franklin stove centerpiece, a small cubbyhole of a bedroom, and an even tinier bathroom with a coffin-sized shower. The bed was a double, wide and too soft. Five extra blankets had been piled at the foot, which didn't say much for the abilities of the wood-burning stove for keeping a sleeper cozy.

Lyanne glanced around the place happily. "This is my favorite of the cabins," the girl confessed. She moved to the window and pushed back the blue gingham curtain. "You've got the best view of the lake from here. Well, other than Adam's room, that is." She waltzed around the room, briefly touching the scarred tabletop and the stained cupboard doors. Lyanne chirped happily, explaining to Kris what kept Klakith Lodge alive. It wasn't fans of Roidan Ryder's world that flocked to the wilderness area. Few of them knew it existed. The place was a haven for fishermen during the summer. They arrived and set up housekeeping in the cabins, bringing their own kitchen utensils. In a curtained alcove were a large sink and a family-sized refrigerator. There was electric power to the cabin. If Kris wished, Lyanne offered to bring a portable television and a VCR down to the cabin. When pressed, though, the young hostess admitted the electricity didn't stretch as far as central heating. Everything was run off a generator and the strain of heating the central lodge was nearly more than it could handle. For keeping warm, the Franklin stove was a wonder, Lyanne promised. Kris just had to give it time to warm up, and keep feeding it.

When Dean drove the BMW up to the door, Kris was tempted to tell him to leave her luggage in the trunk so she could immediately head back down the mountain. But the rental car was parked so that she had a clear view of the dock down at the lake, and the taciturn fisherman who still sat at the end, his dog at his feet. She wouldn't give Adam Cheney or his employer the satisfaction of seeing her take to her heels. She'd grit her teeth and bear this pioneer life. Even if it killed her.

Lyanne was impressed with the amount of luggage Kris had brought with her. Dean grunted under the weight. On his last trip from the car, he handed over the keys Kris had left in the ignition. "There are a couple cardinals out there," he said. "They were cooing at each other on the hood of the Beemer when I got to the lane."

"Cardinals? Oh, that's great!" Lyanne declared.

Kris was beginning to find the girl's enthusiasm a bit wearing.

"That means spring is just around the corner," Lyanne explained. "It's courting time." She gave Dean a shy look that had a good measure of temptress in it. He grinned slowly.

Oh, Lord, Kris thought. *The little minx is looking for a new protector.* Would she find herself in the middle of a jealous battle over the girl? Insane, macho nonsense. The Klakith novels she'd read reeked of the stuff. The sooner she met Roidan Ryder and, if necessary, seduced him away from this damn mountain, the better!

"The only courting I do," Kris said in her most business-like voice, "is for Starburst Pictures and Asteroid Books. If you'd tell Mr. Ryder I'd like to meet with him as soon as . . ."

Lyanne was glowing now, basking under the admiring glance of the young man who had just given a demonstration of brute strength in hefting Kris's luggage in the door. "Oh, Roidan knows you're here, Ms. Jackson. I can't guarantee that he'll talk to you, though. Adam usually handles everything for him."

Who did Roidan Ryder think he was—God? Kris kept a tight rein on her temper. "Then if I can see Mr. Cheney . . ."

Lyanne exchanged a secret glance with Dean. "Oh, you'll see him at dinner," she promised. "It's at seven tonight. I hope that isn't too late."

Given Kris's usual schedule, it was disgustingly early.

"You see," Lyanne added, "I have to see to the horses first."

At Klakith Lodge, Kris wondered, what else could one possibly expect?

four

FROM HER WINDOW, WITH ITS SECOND-BEST VIEW OF THE lake, Kris watched the the gray sky darken. Following Lyanne's lead, she tossed more wood into the stove, but didn't notice any warming of the air in her log cabin. It probably had something to do with the damp breeze that found its way under the heavy plank door. The place hadn't been built for winter use, and had no intention of adapting. Kris had a sneaking suspicion that Adam Cheney knew that.

He was determined to make her leave. Either because Roidan Ryder had instructed him to, or because he didn't like the idea of an out-of-season visitor disturbing his quiet hibernation with his little honey. The discomfort made Kris just as determined to prove she could outlast both Ryder's and Cheney's ill temper. She'd show them she was the champ when it came to being stubborn.

To keep warm, Kris pulled a couple of the ladder-backed chairs away from the table and closer to the Franklin stove.

She piled them with the extra blankets, then, still wrapped in her heavy fur coat, propped her icy feet up next to the warming cast iron. Although turning pages with gloved fingers was a severe test of her temper, Kris whiled the time away by picking up the third Klakith book. As the day darkened she worked her way through a few more of Dalwulf's improbable adventures as he escorted the women of Normass, Reseda, and the Middle World to the marriage mart.

Despite her disenchantment with the subject matter, Roidan Ryder's epics were quick reading. He created the distant world of Klakith with a clarity that made the alien landscape almost familiar. When Dalwulf spoke she now heard the deep timbre of Adam Cheney's voice. When the Dealer soothed one of his lovely companions with a gentle caress, it was Cheney's hand on the head of his Irish setter that Kris saw in her mind's eye. If only the manager of Klakith lodge could be as compassionate as . . .

Kris blinked. She closed the book and stared into the open mouth of the Franklin stove, watching the hungry flames lick the latest batch of wood she'd tossed in.

What a fanciful thought! Dalwulf the Dealer of the planet Klakith was a barbarian who made his living by selling women. How could she think of the character as compassionate?

Kris stared at the cover of the paperback. It showed a scantily clad but extremely blessed woman cowering behind the protective form of a tall, muscular man with long dark red-brown hair and narrowed golden eyes. He was dressed simply as a medieval farmer. Only his physical strength and the gleaming lethal sword in his hand kept the curvaceous woman from being swept away by the evil being that stalked her.

Despite the illustration's coloring, the picture didn't look anything like Adam Cheney. And the pale spring-green complexion of the woman looked nothing like the youthful glowing pink skin of Lyanne. Yet somehow, she could see Cheney and his teen angel in the same stance.

Kris shook off the fanciful notion. She was tired, hungry, and cold. No wonder her mind played tricks on her.

A glance at the Rolex on her wrist showed that it was nearly time for dinner. She wasn't really looking forward to a meal with her reluctant host and bubbly hostess. However, the lodge would be warm. Maybe Lyanne would turn out to be a good cook. Kris put the book down, shoved more wood into the stove on the off chance that the cabin would warm up in her absence, then stepped out into the sting of the night air.

The dilapidated old Chevy truck that belonged to Dean was still parked out front. A trail of fresh tire tracks showed that the Trooper had temporarily found a berth out of the snow at the far end of the lodge in a garage. Kris huddled in her fur and tried to force the wave of depression away. Her own rented car would be frozen in the mud in the morning. She'd probably be frozen in her bed as well. But Adam Cheney's car would be warm and toasty. Such was life at Klakith Lodge.

Although the day had departed, the temperature hadn't dipped just yet. The slush and mud rose up to meet each of Kris's steps, soaking and coating her boots. They'd never be the same after this. They were probably ruined. If they were, Kris was determined to make Joel Halsey pay for a new pair. The whole trip had been his idea. Even if she had jumped at it only to escape dinner at her mother's with a heart specialist.

She stomped her feet to knock the worst of the mud off before pulling open the main door of the lodge. A blast of warm, fragrant air hit her, welcoming Kris inside.

Dean was waiting to take her coat. Briefly Kris feared that he'd hang the fur on the hook behind the door, but the young man produced a coat hanger and hung her wrap in a closet beneath the staircase.

The music was muted this time but only because it came from the kitchen rather than the central sound system. It wasn't Steve Winwood or Def Leppard. Kris strained to identify the sound.

"Can I get you anything to drink, Ms. Jackson?" Dean asked, turning back to her. "We've got tequila, beer, or cola."

A limited selection, to say the least. Kris passed on the offer.

When Dean returned to the kitchen she got a whiff of broiling meat and a louder dose of music. It was easy to recognize the singer. That strong, unfaltering female voice appeared to rise to an emotional shout without the slightest effort. It belonged to only one person. Whitney Houston.

Left alone, Kris mentally sang along with Whitney. She studied the well-read copies of Roidan Ryder's books on the shelves. They'd been arranged in sequence. *The Dealer of Klakith, Brides of Klakith, Prince of Normass, Plains of the Middle World, Dealer's Retreat.* Kris skimmed over the other titles. There were eighteen separate adventures in all, the diligent publication of eight years' worth of Ryder's tales. Even the latest, *The Eve of Kakert*, which had just been released in mid-March, was accounted for in three pristine hardcover copies.

From reading the earlier volumes Kris already knew that the planet Klakith was divided into three separate continents or land masses. The northernmost was called, rather tritely, Normass. It was an overgrown polar cap, a blue-and-white-tinted world that produced humanoid beings with similar coloring. The southern hemisphere tended to gift its landscape and creatures with a pale-green glow and was known as Reseda. Both these lands were separated from the Middle World area by seas that encircled the globe, cut only by the dangerous peninsulas that linked the nations. It was over these treacherous bridges that Dalwulf guided his bevy of beauties to market.

There were two moons circling Klakith. The bluer of the two looped the northern hemisphere; the greener held the south in thrall. Occasionally the mismatched twins merged their orbit, casting a confused but luminescent light over the landscape. It was this night that was considered one of mystery, challenge, and danger . . . the night known as Kakert.

The Middle World viewed the moons as nuisances. Their power came from the red glow of the sun. It allowed the men and women of the equator to have warmer coloring. The reds, browns, and golden tones of Earth thrived there. Kris was just waiting for someone to import women from another planet to the marketplaces of the Middle World. Perhaps in one of the later adventures. So far the stories she'd read had kept within strict confines, never deviating from Ryder's own narrow fantasy world.

A scrape and stomp on the wood flooring startled Kris. Guiltily she looked up from the book through which she'd been thumbing. The illustration on the cover was a little more suggestive than some of the others had been. Dalwulf's large sun-bronzed hand rested intimately against the abdomen of a voluptuous brunette. The vixen seemed to be enjoying the protective embrace, forgetting to act terrified at the sight of the hulking shadow creature just barely discernible in the surrounding gloom. Before anyone could see which volume had held her interest, Kris slid it back into place on the shelf.

In the doorway of the office stood Adam Cheney. "Let me guess," he said. "*Daughter of the Middle World.*"

Kris felt her face flood with color. He'd named the book without the least hesitation.

"Wuella's always been one of my favorite Klakith heroines," he added. His eyes moved over Kris lazily, admiring her lithe figure.

It was Kris's first good look at Cheney as well. He was taller than she'd expected. Nearly six-foot-four. In heels, Kris usually topped the six-foot mark herself. She was used to looking men in the eye, not up at them. His fisherman's sweater made Adam appear broader, but even without its bulk, his shoulders were wide and muscular. His thick red-brown hair curled slightly at the nape of his neck. The glow in his golden eyes was far too warm as it moved over her.

Damn, Kris thought. *He looks more and more like Dalwulf the Dealer.*

Except for the cast, that is.

Adam balanced in the doorway on crutches, his right leg held stiffly. A solid length of plaster rose from his foot and past his knee. One leg of his bark-colored corduroy jeans had been refashioned with a lacing of leather cords to accommodate the injury. The fabric hugged his lean hips and molded snugly to the thigh of his good leg. On his left foot he wore a scuffed Reebok; the right was covered with a heavy cotton athletic sock. The Irish setter appeared at his side, sat down, and leaned against his uninjured leg.

At least the cast explained why he was, to use Lyanne's words, "pretty useless" at the moment.

Adam was glad the crutches were placed solidly. He was afraid he'd make a fool of himself and fall at Kristine Jackson's feet. He'd been anticipating his first good look at her and it proved to be everything he'd feared it would be.

With her short cap of champagne-blond hair, and wide blue eyes, she didn't just resemble Emling of Normass superficially. The damn she-wolf *was* Emling.

He scanned her once from head to foot, then worked his way back up leisurely. Her Amazon height was further enhanced by the tight-fitting black boots. They clung snugly at her ankles, went up a streamlined length of calf and thigh, nearly covering her form-fitting acid-washed jeans. The swashbuckler boots reached nearly to her crotch and were held in place with straps that wove with the belt at her trim waist. He'd only seen one other pair like them, in a rock video with a sultry singer who crooned huskily of "black velvet." Emling had been in the early stages of development when he'd first caught the song on MTV and he'd immediately presented his newest character with a pair.

Kris fulfilled all his other fantasies as well. She was slim, her breasts high but not generous, her bone structure delicate, classic. She was shaped like the overly long sketch of a fashion illustrator. And dramatic as hell. She knew how to carry herself, knew that people would follow her movements with interest and didn't give a damn if they did. The blue of her eyes was dark, as fathomless as the deepest ocean on Klakith, as alluring and cold as the deepest crevasse in the Normass wastelands. Just as he'd imagined Emling to be, Kris Jackson was the ice maiden extraordinaire.

Adam forced himself to move into the room. To look as if she didn't affect him.

"Did Lyanne offer you any refreshments?" he asked, and lowered himself carefully onto one of the leather armchairs. His crutches were set aside, balanced against the bookcase.

The lamplight enhanced the bronze tone of his dark hair, put the feral gleam of his eyes in shadow. The dog followed him across the room and settled at his feet, its head cushioned on his lone Reebok.

Kris sauntered over to the fireplace and stood near the hearth, soaking up the heat and watching the play of flame over the logs. "Dean did," she said. "Is Ryder willing to talk to me?"

Adam shifted in his chair. She was uncommonly direct as well. Like Emling. "Right to the point, huh?"

Kris kept her eyes on the grate. "Let's just say I'll be glad to put this place behind me. I'm here to talk to Ryder. The sooner I do, the sooner you'll be rid of me."

Be rid of a flesh-and-blood Normass maiden? Did he really want that? Where was the irritation he'd felt being goaded into agreeing to Kris's visit? He liked his reputation as a mystery man. Why tamper with a good thing? "Your suite's not up to your usual standards?"

Kris bristled at the insulting tone of his voice. "It wasn't supposed to be, was it? I'm supposed to be frozen out, if not with a cool reception, then with rustic accommodations." She turned, meeting his eyes. "Tell Ryder I'm made of sterner stuff than that."

He scoffed. "A woman who drapes herself in designer-label animal skins? Who hasn't the sense not to drive a BMW up a dirt track? It's a bit difficult to believe you've got a backbone, slick."

The deep blue of her eyes stirred, swirling like an angry whirlpool. Her gently shaped lips thinned. Her jaw tightened. He could almost hear her teeth grind.

He'd hit a nerve, Adam realized, and decided to press a little harder.

"Why don't you just admit it's been a wasted trip? Don't bother to unpack, just load everything up and head hack down the mountain. This isn't your kind of place." He paused a moment and added a final shot. "I'll bet you don't even read Ryder's stuff."

Something lit in her face. Hatred? It was gone in a moment. She was in control. Kris leaned back against the mantelpiece, one three-inch heel hooked on the narrow rise of the bricks around the hearth. "Quiz me," she offered.

Adam smiled slowly. It wasn't a pleasant grin. He was sure he'd catch her. Kris was equally sure she could bluff her way out.

"Planet's name?"

"Klakith," she snapped. "You can get a little more in-depth, Cheney. I didn't start reading them yesterday." Actually, it had been three days since she'd picked up the first volume. But he didn't have to know that.

"Kakert?"

"Holy night. The moons mate."

He'd never phrased it that way, but liked the sound of it. Emling would probably put the interlinking orbits in such terms. In fact, when he got back to his computer, he'd make sure that she did.

"The ruling family of Normass?"

Since she'd just been whiling her time away with *Prince of Normass*, the answer was on the tip of Kris's tongue. "Kipt," she answered as crisply as any rabid Klakithite.

He'd thought he had her on that one. Adam looked thoughtful. "Where's the Valley of Despair?"

Kris backpedaled, trying not to look as cornered as she felt. "Trite name. Hasn't Ryder got a decent imagination?"

Adam's left eyebrow rose in contempt.

"It's on the peninsula," Kris snapped and hoped she'd guessed right.

"Which one?"

Damn. There were two of them. "Aren't convinced yet?" Kris changed tactics. Instead of maintaining a defense, she tried an attack. "Hell, how do I know that you've even read the Klakith chronicles?" she snarled.

Adam didn't pause. "I proofread them," he said.

He would, she stormed silently. "The Valley of Despair is the one on the right," Kris answered, bluffing. "Since you're an expert, just face the correct road."

She didn't know, he thought. But he liked the way she tried to talk her way out of the tight corner.

Adam tried one final broadside. "Who's Tuppence?"

"A character whose name has been stolen from an Agatha Christie book," Kris told him flatly. So much for being brazen. The questions were getting too tough. It was time to turn the tables. "So when do I get to meet Ryder?" she demanded.

Since there were no characters in any of the Klakith stories named Tuppence, Adam was willing to relinquish the game. He'd proved to himself, at least, that she knew little about his novels. But she'd bluffed with a certain finesse that attracted him.

He shrugged in answer to her question. "When he's ready."

"You could point me to his cave," she suggested.

"Even the Kifkows don't live in caves anymore." At her blank look, he explained. "The wild clans of Reseda. On Klakith."

"I know who they are," Kris spat, although she hadn't the least idea what life in Reseda was like. Perhaps the fourth book of the series traveled there. "Has Ryder got some kind of hangup with the letter *K*? There's the Kifkows, Kakert, Klakith . . ."

"The river Ku, Mount Kaept, the Kobleck Sea, the Kilstem ridge, the . . ."

Kris interrupted the flow of imaginary geographical features. "Ryder will like me," she said.

"Why is that, slick?" Adam asked patiently.

Kris smiled smugly at him. "Because I belong on Klakith," she purred. "My name begins with one of those blessed, blasted K's of which Ryder's so fond."

Adam choked off a bark of laughter. "Perhaps you do belong on Klakith, after all," he murmured in amusement.

five

BELONGING ON KLAKITH AND MEETING THE CREATOR OF the planet and its inhabitants were two entirely different subjects, Kris found when Lyanne called them to dinner moments later.

They ate in the kitchen merely because that was the only place to eat. There was no formal dining done at Klakith Lodge. Adam Cheney's home was the center of a summer fishing village. It had none of the luxuries found in a royal Normass manor.

Kris was used to more sophisticated surroundings. The round, highly buffed oak table was set for four. Quilted forest-green oval placemats designated the seating. Stark white Corelle ware, tall Libby glasses with a blue-green design, and hollow-handle colonial-looking stainless steel flatware were all arranged with Amy Vanderbilt precision. Hurricane lamps glowed warmly in the center of the table and on the counters.

Dean held a ladder-backed chair, indicating where Kris was to sit. Adam leaned his crutches against the wall and arranged his leg beneath the table, balancing his foot on the claw-footed base. Although a guest should have been seated on his right, Kris was on Adam's left. Lyanne took the chair across from her, explaining that she didn't want Adam's cast to get in Kris's way.

Cheney grinned evilly at Kris, as if he knew she was thinking how much she would have enjoyed kicking the plaster when he infuriated her.

"Only four places? Isn't Mr. Ryder joining us?"

Lyanne set serving bowls on neat trivets and took her seat. Dean began passing the food. There was a platter of T-bone steaks, baked potatoes, a bowl of buttered corn, and another of tossed salad. Kris made sure she got her share of everything. They might try to freeze her out, but she wasn't going to let them starve her as well.

"Roidan doesn't eat with us. Not if he can help it," Lyanne said. She glanced at Adam.

"He had other plans," Cheney said.

It looked like no one talked to Roidan Ryder directly. Everything was channeled through his agent, Adam Cheney. Kris cut into her steak and was chagrined to find it was cooked to an even browness. She might have guessed this bunch would be unable to appreciate a fine rare steak.

Dean sprinkled his own meat liberally with steak sauce before savoring a bite. He grinned across the table at Cheney. "Ryder probably had a hot date with Emling."

Adam's red-earth brows joined over the bridge of his nose as he frowned.

Lyanne glared at Dean as well. "Ix-nay on Emling," she hissed.

Kris was dying to know who Emling was now. But something else distracted her. Her fork suspended part-way between plate and mouth, Kris stared at her hosts.

Those furious expressions were too identical for one of them to be a lover's unconscious imitation. She compared, her eyes moving between two heads of reddish hair, one dark, one bright. Between two pair of golden eyes, one deep amber, one honey. There was nothing similar in their build. Adam was the essence of a barbarian giant, muscular, fierce. Lyanne was delicate, willowy, blessed with generous curves. Yet . . .

The truth dawned on Kris. Lyanne wasn't Adam Cheney's live-in love. His "assistant" was his sister!

Kris stabbed another piece of steak. She kept her eyes lowered to her plate. "You should have invited this Emling to dinner as well," she said. Only Cheney seemed to notice her voice was just shy of a growl. His stormy expression cleared, replaced by a smirk of amusement.

Lyanne's brow puckered in confusion. "Invite Emling to dinner? How . . . ?" She glanced to her brother.

"To get Roidan Ryder to come as well," he explained. "Ms. Jackson doesn't understand the . . . er . . . difficulty involved in that. Pass the butter, would you, Dean?"

Eating was beyond Kris at the moment. She put her fork down as the butter dish crossed the table. "Is the difficulty in luring Ryder? Or is this Emling tied up?"

"Tied up?" Adam seemed to savor the idea a moment. Or perhaps it was the forkful of butter-drenched potato. "Not at the moment, she's not."

Dean made a sound. Like a stifled burst of laughter. His eyes brimmed with amusement. "Tempting though, isn't it?" he asked.

Adam's gaze rested briefly on Kris before he applied himself to his steak. "Very," he said with heartfelt sincerity.

Dean sputtered anew.

Feeling very out of the conversation, Kris hid her irritation and lifted her glass. It contained nothing more exciting than ice water. Lyanne had a tall glass of milk, but that didn't appeal to Kris. Dinner without a glass of wine seemed barbaric.

But things at Klakith Lodge *were* barbaric compared to the civilized world. She'd make Joel Halsey pay dearly for coming up with this assignment.

Kris put her drink down. "Is Emling Ryder's sweetheart? Somebody else's wife? What's the problem? What is this Emling like?"

Dean smiled slowly. "Actually," he said, his glance studying Kris thoroughly, "she's an awful lot like you."

"She's a character in the last two books," Adam explained. "Ryder's on a deadline, you know. It was ridiculous of anyone to think he could take time out to promote anything. Even if he was inclined to do so."

Kris wasn't listening very closely to Cheney's gripe. "What do you mean, the last two books? The last ones published? Or the last of the series?"

"If you'd read the most recent release," Adam chided, "you'd already know the answer. Emling's a character that first appears in the nineteenth volume, which won't be out for another six months."

Kris was the one whose brow was furrowed in thought now. "So it's been turned in? The editor has read it?"

Adam noticed her careful phrasing. "Of course they've read it. I went over the copyedited version this week."

"So Asteroid Books knows what Emling looks like?" Kris persisted.

"Yeah," Cheney said, drawing the word out, his voice now suspicious.

Kris was still narrowing things down. "And she looks like me?"

"Of course not," Lyanne insisted. "Emling's got blue skin!"

"The SOB's," Kris growled. "No wonder everyone was determined to send me to this godforsaken place!"

Dean paused in the act of shoveling a forkful of corn into his mouth. "Are you kidding? This is God's country!"

Kris gave him a withering look. Rutted muddy roads, snow, and freezing temperatures were not her idea of the Creator's master plan. "I'd rather be stretched out on a deck chair in the Caribbean."

He chewed thoughtfully. "Now that you mention it," Dean said, "that sounds one hell of a lot better to me, too."

Cheney had given up all pretense of eating. His chair scratched back across the floor as he hefted his cast from beneath the table. He looked like a man who needed to pace. Instead, his fingers drummed impatiently on the tabletop. "Are you saying the publicity people chose you merely because of your surface resemblance to a fictional character?"

Her appetite ruined, Kris pushed her plate away. "I was vain enough to think it was because I was competent."

Only the younger couple continued to enjoy their meal. While Kris and Adam glared at their own barely touched plates, Lyanne offered Dean flirtatious smiles and hot apple pie.

Adam scowled, unaware when Lyanne gave the generous remains of his steak to the overjoyed Irish setter. He barely noticed when his sister and Dean eased out of the room.

Damn, he raged silently. For once he wished he'd developed a more profane vocabulary to express the frustration he felt. But a man with a precocious little sister to bring up had to watch what he said. The restraint forced him to fall back on expressions he'd created for Klakithites, and for the first time in his life they didn't suffice.

Slumped in his chair, Adam transferred his malevolent gaze to Kris. If he believed her, she'd been hoodwinked into thinking her expertise in handling reluctant celebrities was required to convince the reclusive Roidan Ryder onto the publicity circuit. Had it been more her resemblance to Emling that had qualified her for the assignment, though? It was uncanny that she should be so very like the Normass maiden. Lyanne had lit hurricane lamps around the room, preferring the softer glow of the flickering flames to the harsh glare of the overhead electric lights. In the dim light he could almost believe that Kris was Emling. He'd already described how the illumination of a campfire made Emling's pale cerulean skin warmer, almost golden. Closer to the soft, alluring glow of Kris Jackson's complexion.

He studied her high cheekbones, the shape of her brows as they drew together in fury over her impossibly straight nose. Her lips were thinned at the moment. He wondered what they would be like when she smiled. Would the edges curve slightly in amusement or stretch widely in welcome? Would they feel soft to the touch? And, perhaps, more importantly, how would she taste when he kissed her? Because if Kris Jackson was around much longer, Adam knew he would kiss her.

"And are you competent?" he asked.

"I thought so," Kris said. "Until now, that is." She smiled, but bitterly. "All those whistle stops. Lord, and I was just window dressing!"

She was too sure of herself to be nothing but a long-legged blond, though. Adam pressed for more information. "How many whistle stops?"

Kris looked up, met the interrogating look in his feral eyes. "Lots. Too many. What the hell does it matter?"

He surprised her by smiling. "Perhaps you were chosen for this particular job because of your looks," he said. "What I want to know is, were they the only reason?"

"You want to see my resumé, is that it? Lord, you're a careful bastard, Cheney. Afraid I'll give Mr. Meal Ticket Ryder a taste of the outside world and take over your job?"

"Just tell me who you've worked with," he suggested.

She stared at him a moment longer before shrugging and sitting up straighter in her chair. "Didn't Dean say something about some tequila?"

"In the pantry. Glasses top left cupboard. Bring me one, too, if you don't mind."

With Adam's directions, Kris soon had shot glasses, limes, salt, and the bottle of tequila on the table. He cut the limes, filled the glasses, and offered her first chance at the salt shaker.

"I am qualified," she said, before running through the ceremony. Gulp of tequila, a suck on the lime, a kiss of salt from the back of her hand. She mentioned a few names—actresses, composers, celebrities—then added, "I just came off three months with Dead Heat."

Adam nodded. Lyanne had shown him the picture in the magazine. Studying it, he'd had a fleeting, unreasonable urge to smash Tasker Fane's teeth in. "Heavy metal group. I doubt if they were reluctant to greet their fans."

"Reluctant? No," Kris admitted. "With them it was a case of being not reluctant enough. Do you know how many underage girls there are out there who look much older?"

"Like my sister, for instance?"

"Yes." Kris was pleased to have a verification of his relationship with Lyanne. She still didn't like Adam Cheney, she told herself, but it was nice to know he wasn't as stupid as she'd originally thought. "My job was to keep the group visible but not allow them to get out of hand."

Adam grimaced as he bit down on a slice of lime. "And did you?"

Kris watched the fluid smoothness of his movements as Adam sprinkled fresh salt on the back of his hand and then sucked it off. "Don't you mean, how did I do it?" she asked.

He grinned. "Don't spoil my fantasies, slick. I'm sure you did whatever was necessary."

She ground her teeth in irritation. "That damn picture! What do you think this job entails? Sleeping with the clients? Is that what Ryder wants to know?"

"Isn't it a logical assumption?"

Kris growled. She reached for the bottle of tequila and refilled her shot glass. "That's just the attitude I would expect. All you have to do is read the Klakith stories to know Ryder has a low opinion of women. If you didn't feel the same way, you wouldn't have been with him so long."

Adam sat up straighter in his chair. He leaned forward, his attitude one of suppressed violence. "Where the hell did you get an asinine idea like that?"

"What? That Ryder's a creep and you're probably one by association?" Tequila, lime, salt. Kris glared at him through each step. "What's the problem? Ryder doesn't want me here anyway. And neither do you."

It was the tequila that made her reckless. Her blue eyes were a bit glazed, her cheeks a bit brighter. "I'm sure you have your uses," Adam said, fueling her anger by giving Kris a languid look that lingered on the outline of her breasts beneath her sweater.

"Barbarian. It just so happens it takes diplomacy to get people with inflated egos to behave decently."

"A virtuous trait I can see you excel at," he murmured. "It's quite fascinating to see the way you temper the insults through diplomacy."

Knowing she'd yet to be subtle with anyone at Klakith Lodge, Kris leaned on the table and played with a fresh slice of lime. "I haven't felt the need to go easy on you, Cheney. It's Ryder I was sent to deal with."

"Ah, but you need me to get to him," Adam pointed out. "You really should be nicer to me."

She sucked on the lime, without the tequila this time, measuring him as she did so. "Does Emling cozy up to Dalwulf?"

Surprised at her question, Adam laughed. "As a matter of fact, yes, she does."

"Dream on, buster," Kris recommended. "Just because I'm the image of this Normass peahen doesn't mean I want to have anything to do with Dalwulf's double."

The Dealer's doppelganger grinned. "You think I look like Dalwulf?"

"Don't be coy. You know you do, Cheney. Hell, how close are you and Ryder? Blood brothers?"

"Sort of," Adam said. He filled his shot glass one last time, then capped the bottle of tequila. "You see, I am Roidan Ryder."

six

KRIS PAUSED. THEN SHE SNORTED. "HA! TELL ME AN-other one. The Klakith tales have been around for nearly ten years. You aren't old enough to have written them."

"I'm thirty," Adam said.

She would have thought him a few years younger. "See, too young," Kris claimed. "Introduce me to the real Roidan Ryder. I promise not to spoil your setup here."

Adam leaned back in his chair, tilting it a bit to balance on the back legs. For a man with one limb in a cast, he lived dangerously. "Ever hear of Terry Brooks?"

Kris leaned back in her chair as well, her long leather-clad legs stretched out, ankles crossed. Elbows on the arms of her chair, she laced her fingers together over her stomach. "Nope. Never heard of him. Is that Ryder's real name?"

"You have a one-track mind," Adam complained. Her stance was making his run on a fairly narrow track as well—one that had nothing to do with the Klakith tales or publicity for the movie. It had just been too damn long since he'd taken one of his sabbaticals to the city. Ostensibly they were for research, but a week in town without Lyanne also meant the possibility of an evening or two with a warm female body next to his in bed.

"Brooks is a writer of fantasy novels," Adam explained. "He wrote his first Shannara stories when he was in his teens."

"Which proves?"

Adam shifted his injured leg in irritation. "Nothing to you, apparently."

Kris shrugged. "What's your point?"

"That it's not age but ability that makes a writer."

Her lips twisted in a smirk. "Come on. Most writers don't make it till they're on the wrong side of forty. It takes life experience to portray a variety of emotions and actions."

"Don't talk statistics to me. Or life experience." The memory of a tangled mass of steel on the freeway and a frightened little girl's face surfaced briefly in his mind. "It doesn't take time to live through hell."

Kris's smug grin was more pronounced now. Adam wished he had the agility to pin her in the chair and kiss the skepticism away. The weight of the damn cast held him back. "I write the Klakith books," he said quietly. "I created the planet, the people, the society."

"Good try, Cheney," Kris allowed. "Now, when do I get to meet Ryder?"

Lyanne Cheney leaned against the stall door, her arms loosely draped over Dean Taggart's shoulders. Behind them a pinto stood dozing, its head nodding slightly. The Irish setter had made herself a bed in the hay and rested, waiting for her mistress to return to the warmth of the main lodge.

The girl's pastel ski jacket was open. Dean's work-roughened hands were spread possessively along her ribs as he bent his head to the pleasant task of kissing her. Lyanne returned each caress of his lips with equal enthusiasm and pleasure. He pressed her back against the wooden door, his body hard and eager for hers. Lyanne sighed happily and wiggled closer to him.

When they both came up for air, her honey-shaded eyes were glowing. But it wasn't praise for his expertise that fell from her lips. Lyanne's body might be responding to his, but Dean knew, after nearly five months together, that the girl's nimble mind jumped to subjects that had nothing to do with him. He wasn't surprised that, while snuggled closely to him, she was already thinking about something else.

"She's perfect, isn't she?" Lyanne murmured.

Dean's mind was still a bit distracted by the way her young, lush body brushed against his. "Who?" He nibbled lightly on Lyanne's earlobe.

"Ms. Jackson." The girl responded to his caresses by running her fingers through his hair.

Knowing he had to maintain his end of the conversation, at least until his girlfriend could be distracted back to the pleasure of these stolen moments, Dean mumbled a response against Lyanne's collarbone. "Perfect for what?"

"For whom, silly. She's perfect for Adam, of course."

"Ah," Dean agreed, and returned to his self-appointed task.

"It's long past time that he got married," Lyanne said, perfectly able to carry on a conversation while Dean's lips grazed over her skin.

"Maybe he doesn't want to get married," Dean suggested. "Not everyone is as old-fashioned as I am."

Lyanne grinned fondly at him. "I know," she purred. "But Adam would never agree to our getting married until I'm older. Maybe when I'm eighteen he'll be more agreeable."

Dean pulled back from her arms and cupped her face. Briefly he kissed her one last time. "I wish you'd let me talk to him. This is sheer hell, Lye."

She caressed his cheek. "I know," she soothed. "But if Adam would just fall in love himself, everything would be so much easier."

"Yeah, sure," Dean groaned. "He doesn't think I'm good enough for you."

Lyanne giggled. "Of course not. He's my brother."

"More like your father. He's a lot more suspicious of me than any brother would be."

"You don't know Becky's older brother, do you?" she teased. "He's worse than her father when it comes to her dating."

Dean picked up a curry brush and let himself into the adjacent stall. The tall bay gelding that belonged to Adam Cheney nuzzled him in greeting. He'd been exercising the horse ever since Adam's accident the previous fall. Now grooming the gelding's reddish coat was easier on his libido than holding Lyanne much longer.

"We aren't just dating, Lye. I love you. I've asked you to marry me," Dean said.

Lyanne rested her chin on the stall door. "And we will get married," she promised. "In two years."

The brush moved along the horse's back in smooth even strokes. "It's getting harder to stop myself every time we're together."

She frowned. "I won't do anything to destroy Adam's trust. You know that. I thought you respected my feelings."

"I know, I know." Although his intentions were honorable, he wouldn't push her to consummate their love until Lyanne herself was ready. Her body was that of a woman, but there was still a good bit of little girl housed within it.

"Maybe I should stay away for awhile," he suggested. "Adam gets the cast off this week. He'll be able to handle things around here again. I'll spend more time with the band. See if we can't get it together, play a few gigs."

He was a bit disappointed when she didn't look heartbroken.

"That's great!" Lyanne declared. "And while you're doing that, I'll work on getting Adam and Ms. Jackson married."

Dean frowned. "I don't know. Aren't you getting carried away? What makes you think they even like each other?"

"The electricity between them! Couldn't you feel it?"

"I thought that was disgust."

Lyanne's stiffly sprayed plume of copper bangs waved. "Of course they don't trust each other. It's part of the attraction. Adam didn't want New York to send anybody out but he couldn't refuse them. Not with the contract pending for the new series. You know they just want more Klakith stuff and he wants Dalwulf to retire. Ms. Jackson probably doesn't know about that since she's here about movie promotion. But she sees Adam as an obstacle in getting to Roidan Ryder. With both of them so negative, it had to be a case of hatred at first sight!"

Dean still wasn't convinced. "Where did you get a weird idea like that?"

Lyanne was affronted. "From reading, of course!"

"Those trashy romances that Becky gives you?"

She looked sly now. The expressions flitted quickly across her mobile little face. "Not from those books. And they aren't trashy. They're just slices of life."

Dean snorted. The horse snorted. The dog sneezed.

"Well, they are," Lyanne insisted. "But it was from reading the Klakith books that I learned about the kind of attraction that would work for Adam."

"You think that just because Kris Jackson looks like Emling that he'll be drooling over her?"

Lyanne sniffed. "My brother doesn't drool over women," she said stiffly. "And she doesn't look *exactly* like Emling. Normass women have blue skin, you know."

"Technicality. She's got everything else."

"Including those bitchin' boots," Lyanne agreed with a touch of envy. "All I have to do is keep her here long enough and nature will take care of the rest."

"Don't count on it," Dean recommended. "If Adam was interested in getting married he would have found a wife already. Instead he just takes those trips to the city to *research*."

Lyanne's eyes widened. "What do you mean? He gathers details for the stories."

Dean laughed at that. "What kind of research can be done on a planet he invented? Everything that happens on Klakith is a result of his imagination."

"If you are implying that my brother *pays* for . . ."

"Not a bit. With his looks, all Adam has to do is look vaguely interested and women fall all over him."

Lyanne wasn't willing to accept the story yet. "If that were the case, then why . . ."

"Isn't there a path from town to your door? Because he isn't interested in an enduring relationship, baby. Some men don't want to be tied to one woman." Dean finished brushing the bay's glowing coat. He put the curry brush aside but didn't leave the stall just yet. "You know my aunt?"

"Doyle's mother?"

"Naw, the younger one. Roxie. Remember when she was here visiting after her divorce?"

Lyanne was thoughtful. "Yes," she said carefully. If she remembered correctly, Roxie Taggart was a very shapely brunette. She wasn't that much older than Dean, despite the fact that she was his father's little sister. Roxie had come to Klakith with Dean one day last fall. The woman said she wanted too meet Lyanne but she hadn't spent much time with the girl. Instead, Roxie had taken her cup of coffee into Adam's office and chattered to him for over an hour.

"Well, Roxie would have given her eyeteeth for Adam to call her," Dean said. "She dropped hints like crazy, but he never gave her even a wink."

The visit with Dean's pushy aunt now clear in her mind, Lyanne was more inclined to think her brother had excellent taste in ignoring the woman.

"But Ms. Jackson is different," she insisted. "She's got a chip on her shoulder. Like . . . like . . ." There were so many Klakith heroines who had opposed Dalwulf or the councils of Normass, Reseda, and the Middle World. "Like Wuella," Lyanne said. "In *Daughter of the Middle World* she doesn't like the idea of having to marry the heir to Reseda's generalship. She doesn't like the idea that Wulfy is just as determined to deliver her to the palace. And since they're at odds, Wulfy falls for her." Lyanne grinned widely, sure that she'd found the key to what would make her brother happy. "It's the same with Ms. Jackson and Adam, only in this case she's been sent to bring *him* back."

Dean's expression was gloomy. "Just because he wrote a story where that happened doesn't mean that . . ."

Lyanne was convinced. "Yes, it does." She frowned briefly, chewing her lip in thought. "Do you think she'd mind if I start calling her Kris? I mean, if she's going to be my sister-in-law, it doesn't sound right to call her Ms. Jackson."

seven

UNAWARE THAT HER FUTURE WAS BEING PLOTTED FOR her, Ms. Jackson was huddled in her cabin, in front of the open door of the Franklin stove, counting the freezing hours until dawn. There was no way anyone was going to get her to sleep in the icy bedroom. The thought of a morning shower was far from appealing under these conditions; she'd probably turn blue if she tried.

Which would make her look even more like Emling of Normass.

Damn Joel Halsey! She still couldn't believe that he'd had the nerve to send her off on this wild-goose chase just because she resembled a character in a book. Yet it was just the kind of thing he'd do. *Mission Impossible* had always been his favorite show, and the kind of assignments he liked best were those that resembled the incredible expeditions Jim Phelps headed.

It was one thing to be manipulated when she knew all

the facts. But Halsey had held out on her.

From her work with other authors, Kris knew that there was a long lead time from when a completed manuscript was turned in and when it hit the shelves at the bookstore. Because they were so popular, Asteroid Books rushed Roidan Ryder's epics through the system. Within nine months of the time he finished writing a story, it was bound and in the book racks. In comparison, most writers were looking at a year to two years before they could contemplate any autograph sessions.

Asteroid's editor had told her that Ryder was working on the twentieth adventure for Dalwulf and his minions. It was due in at the end of May. By then they would have pumped the nineteenth story through copyediting and into galley form. The dustcover was in its final stages. They'd shown Kris a mock-up. Same old hero, same luscious babe, same hulking shadowy threat. Only the titles and the stances changed.

Now she wondered if they hadn't shown her the wrong illustration in a further cover-up of their real intention in choosing her for the trip. The heroine in jeopardy on that cover hadn't been tall, blond, or blue-eyed. She'd been petite, brunette, and moon-faced.

Which moon? The blue Normass one or the green Reseda one?

Lord! She was really in bad shape. She was even thinking in Klakith terms now!

Kris peeled off her boots and sat them close to the stove to dry out. Imagine! Cheney had thought to brush her off with that whopper about his being Roidan Ryder. The man would try anything to get rid of her.

Of course he and Ryder had cooked up that little lie to protect Ryder's identity. What was wrong with the man? Was Roidan Ryder scarred from some horrible accident?

Deformed at birth? For all she knew, the Elephant Man wrote the Klakith adventures!

Creating the impression that Adam Cheney wrote the stories had obviously been their plan all along. Ryder had seen the necessity to have a front man at the start and had hired Cheney because he looked like Dalwulf the Dealer. After all, the public would probably expect to see Ryder as a man who looked like the hero of Klakith.

But Kris wasn't gullible enough to believe their story. It irked her that they would think she was, and that she would accept Cheney as her partner on the publicity tour. He could blithely sign Ryder's name and no one would be the wiser. Except her.

It didn't matter how much the Cheneys tried to freeze her, she wasn't going to budge until she could ferret out Roidan Ryder himself and drag him, screaming if necessary, down the mountain and on tour.

Once she got him back to civilization though, Kris was damned if she had any intention of working the schedule of appearances herself. If the creator of Dalwulf couldn't hold his own among the real wolves, well . . . tough!

It was war now. Pure and simple. She knew more about the enemy, in the form of Adam Cheney and the manipulative powers of Roidan Ryder. Once she read the complete history of Klakith she'd know even more about how Ryder thought. And for Cheney? Well, she'd just have to swallow her pride and infiltrate his little hideaway. The best person to use toward that end was his little sister, the obnoxiously eager Lyanne. It was despicable, Kris knew, to even consider such a two-faced plan. Desperate people used desperate measures, though. If the idea of getting out from under Adam Cheney's disturbing feral glance wasn't reason enough for fast action, the cold that was creeping into her bones was!

Kris stripped the pillows and blankets from the bed and built a nest near the stove. Then, surrounded by the Klakith novels she'd pilfered from the lodge while Adam was still in the kitchen, she settled down to the business of psyching out Roidan Ryder.

Adam lay on his back in bed, his arms bent, hands behind his head, and stared at the ceiling. She hadn't believed him. It was the first time he'd confessed to being Roidan Ryder, and Kris Jackson had just smirked, her expression as good as calling him a liar.

His dual identity wasn't a secret in Cedar City. The people that Lyanne hadn't told had discovered the secret in other ways. The postmaster knew because the publisher always addressed everything to Ryder. The town tax office knew that it was his name on the deed to the lodge property. Even his checks at the bank carried both names, blatantly admitting that Adam Cheney did business under the name Roidan Ryder.

But the living, breathing clone of Emling didn't believe he wrote the Klakith epics.

Adam smiled at the rafters. The ceiling in the upstairs was slanted, rising to a peak that centered over the hallway between both bedrooms. He'd designed the lodge, creating separate areas for Lyanne and himself. His sister's room was to the back, her windows giving onto a view of tall pine trees and the peaceful clearing where their horses grazed. His own suite faced the lake and had a balcony where he could sit and enjoy the stars during the summer months.

It seemed a century ago that he'd sat in the narrow window of his apartment in Los Angeles and promised himself that he'd give Lyanne back the stars. Would strive to give her everything he'd had growing up in a small country town. He'd done more than re-create that idyllic existence.

He still found it amazing that he'd accomplished it so easily.

Now that a life of scraping by was so far in his past, Adam barely recalled the tension of those years. He'd thought things were coming to a peak when he received a promotion to credit manager at the bank and been transferred to Riverside, California. Although the smog of the city rolled in and hovered over the smaller town, caught by the height of the San Bernardino Mountains at its back, he had thought they could be happy there.

The sale of the house back in Illinois had corresponded to the move and he'd been able to purchase a small house within walking distance of the Victoria Elementary School. He'd even looked into returning to school evenings at the University of California campus in Riverside. Everything had been perfect.

Even his love life.

Adam sighed, his mind trying to dredge up a complete picture of Margaret. . . . What had Maggie's last name been? Leach . . . Lear? Leigh! Imagine that. The woman he'd once considered marrying, and he had trouble remembering her name.

Or what she looked like. She'd been Lyanne's teacher. A lovely young woman in her first year in the school system. There had still been an aura of the college campus about her. Perhaps that was what had appealed to him. Only success with his writing had killed the pain of forsaking his own career in academics.

What else could he remember about Maggie? Her smile? In his usually fertile imagination, the picture wouldn't come. The feel of her in his arms? Nothing. Basic things, then. Like the color of her eyes? A mysteriously shaded blue danced in his mind. As deeply tinged as the depths of a lake. Not

Maggie's coloring, or even Emling's. But it was the exact shade of Kris Jackson's eyes.

He pushed the vision away. It was dangerous to spend any time dwelling on that woman. She was a princess of the city. Every inch of her shouted the influence of money, what possession of it could accomplish, what . . .

Accomplish? Perhaps things could be accomplished without the lure of greenbacks. All one needed was the right bait.

He heard the loud burst of sound as Dean Taggart's Ford came back to life. The roar of the motor destroyed the peace and quiet of the forest before dwindling into the distance as the young man made his way back down the mountain to town.

Lyanne was very impressed with Kris Jackson. Adam wasn't sure whether her enthusiasm was tied to the woman's past as a model or to her acquaintance with Tasker Fane and the rest of the Dead Heat musicians. Whichever it was, he had a suspicion that if Kris told Lyanne something, the girl would take it as gospel. Whereas if he laid down the same law, he would be considered unreasonable.

Across the hall he could hear the music already blasting. Who was it this time? He tried to keep up with Lyanne's enthusiasms, but she'd taken such a drastic turn in her tastes in the last few months that she'd left him behind. When he'd mentioned his concern to her best friend Becky's mother, the woman had just laughed. "Your little girl is growing up, Adam. You've got to let go sometime." Now was not the time, though. Not with Lyanne suddenly blooming into womanhood and Dean Taggart panting at her heels in appreciation. Adam was afraid that curiosity alone would lead his sister into giving herself to Taggart.

He might have wanted to let Lyanne enjoy the same joys he'd had before going off to college, but he was chauvinistic enough to draw the line at sex. For a moment, remembering his own youthful, heated fumblings brought him back to contemplating Kris Jackson's exciting form . . .

Adam sighed and sat up. This wasn't going to be easy. Not if Kris actually took him up on the deal he was considering offering her in the morning. But if it worked, perhaps it would be worth every frustrating moment of having the woman around. Besides, once the cast came off on Monday, he'd be able to take cold showers again. For now, it was the freezing bite of the great outdoors.

Crutches in place, Adam worked his way over to the wide patio doors and slid one back. The stars twinkled far above. The breeze had dropped but its bite was still sufficient to sting his cheeks. For once, though, the cold didn't work its magic on his blood. The light spilling from Kris Jackson's cabin was much too bright a reminder of her presence.

eight

THE MUSIC WAS LOUD ENOUGH TO SET HIS OFFICE WALLS pulsing to the beat.

"_Turn down the damn music!_" Adam bellowed for perhaps the fourth time.

This time his sister heard him. She danced into view. She stood framed in the open doorway, her hips still moving to the steady throb of the drums. "You can't _not_ like Aerosmith," she shouted over the song.

"That's a double negative."

Lyanne ignored his automatic correction of her grammar. "Even grandmothers like Aerosmith, Adam," she insisted.

It was time he killed the satellite dish. Lyanne was even talking like the hosts on MTV.

He really should be used to the sound of heavy metal music by now. Every weekday morning the first sign his sister gave that she was awake was the sound of MTV blaring from the television set in her room. She sang and danced along to the music videos as she got ready to go down the mountain to school. Because this was Saturday, there had been a slight delay in the ruckus merely because Lyanne slept an hour or two longer. But once the sun had arrived in the sky, so had the harsh growl of the music.

He felt old complaining about it. After all, Adam admitted reluctantly, the volume on his own music was rarely muted below a roar. It was their tastes that differed.

Hell! In spite of his intentions, he found himself sounding more and more like his parents when dealing with Lyanne. Circumstances had made him ancient before his time.

Lyanne turned, dancing away from his office and back into the main living area. Adam ignored the flashing cursor on the screen of his IBM-PC. He'd meant to work a little more, polishing the last chapter he'd written before diving into the action planned in the next one. Usually he was further along in the story at this point. The deadline was closing in, with less than two months to go. Which could be more than enough time under some circumstances. The current circumstances weren't exactly perfect. Not only did his worries about Lyanne distract him, but the plans he'd made concerning Kris Jackson put him off stride as well.

Face it, Adam told himself. It was going to be next to impossible to work until he put the plan into action.

He tilted his chair back and watched his sister dance in and out of the limited view afforded by his office doorway. In two years she'd be ready to go off to college. He'd put the thought off, preferring not to face that distant future. But it wasn't that far away anymore. What would he do when she left? Would he follow, moving to whichever campus she chose? Or would he stay at the lodge, dividing his time between fishing and writing? He had delayed having a future of his own for so long now that it was difficult to even consider having one separate from that of his little sister.

What were the advantages? The disadvantages? It had been six years since he'd noticed the ad for the lodge in the listing for out-of-town property in the Riverside newspaper. The royalties on his first Klakith adventures had come in and a neighbor had mentioned being interested in buying Adam's home if he was planning on selling in the near future. Margaret had just broken off their relationship as well, and he'd had a succession of bad days at the bank. The circumstances all seemed geared toward pushing him to move. So he had.

Lyanne had adapted as only a ten-year-old could. She'd been uprooted enough in the move from Illinois, then from one neighborhood to another as he tried to better their standard of living. Her resentment at having to move from a neighborhood crowded with kids to the loneliness of the cabin hadn't lasted much past the arrival of her first pony. And with a brother who wasn't tied to the specific regime of an office clock, it had been easy to arrange to visit her school friends whenever she chose or have them come up to the lodge. Once the parents of Lyanne's friends discovered that Adam was an overly conscientious guardian, the lodge had become the local playground.

And so life had fallen into a daily round of going back and forth between Cedar City and the cabin.

He'd miss it when she left. But he'd never thought to hold her in the mountains. He would be disappointed if Lyanne decided to marry a local boy and thus miss seeing any of the outside world.

Which brought his thoughts back to Dean Taggart and Lyanne's recent adoption of short, tight skirts and off-the-shoulder blouses.

And that in turn made him think of Kris Jackson.

During a break in the music he heard the front door open and Kris's voice as she greeted Lyanne. It was time to put his plan into action.

Kris Jackson poked her head around the door before entering. "Hey! Isn't that Aerosmith?"

Lyanne grinned happily at her visitor, her dancing temporarily halted while the cassette ran the rest of the tape out before automatically switching to the second side. In a swift glance she took in Kris's outfit. Today their visitor wore a gray, brown, and rust-patterned sweater with pleated slate-colored corduroy trousers and short brown boots. "You like Aerosmith?" Lyanne sounded incredulous.

Already set on making fast friends with the teenager, Kris nodded. She moved farther into the room and perched on one of the wooden settees. "Doesn't everyone?"

Lyanne curled up comfortably on the adjacent bench. She had chosen to wear a baggy, black plaid flannel shirt over a glow-in-the-dark green Danskin and matching leggings. Her cotton socks were black as well and bunched around her slim ankles. Lyanne's nose wrinkled. "I don't think Adam cares much for them," she said.

Feeling that slamming Adam Cheney's taste in music was not the approach she needed to take, Kris ignored Lyanne's complaint. At least it was wonderfully warm in the main lodge. She hoped she didn't look too distracted by the crackling heat of the blazing fire. "Did you get to see Aerosmith when they opened the Hard Rock Cafe in Las Vegas? After all, Vegas is not that far away."

"Wouldn't I have loved to!" Lyanne sighed. The stereo blasted back to life, but the teenager surprised Kris by turning down the sound. "You know what tickets cost for the show?" she demanded, her mind still on the missed opportunity to see Aerosmith in person. "I heard they were $250 apiece."

"They were," Kris said. "I was there for the first show. They built a temporary shelter, a tent sort of thing to house the show. But anybody who could get through the traffic and sit on the adjacent empty lots or business properties could hear the show for free. They just couldn't see it."

"Wow!" Lyanne breathed in awe. "You've done everything, haven't you."

It wasn't a question but a statement filled with longing.

"So will you," Kris assured her. "After all, I hadn't done anything when I was . . . how old are you, anyway?"

"Sixteen."

Good grief! Just a baby! Kris would never have guessed that voluptuous figure belonged to any girl so young.

"I didn't have a horse or live on a mountain lake, either," Kris said, hoping she sounded envious. The view of Central Park from her apartment was as close as she had ever wanted to get to serious contemplation of Mother Nature. "What bands have you seen?" she asked.

Lyanne's face fell. "None!" she declared, her voice pitched low to emphasize the true tragedy of the pronouncement. "No one plays Cedar City. At least, no one famous!"

Kris commiserated and wondered where Adam Cheney was hiding. She didn't want him to overhear, and possibly guess what she was up to. He probably wouldn't look kindly on her making friends with his sister. Especially since she had every intention of exploiting the girl's naive trust to wangle her way to Roidan Ryder's hiding place.

"Of course, Dean's band is good," Lyanne said.

Ah, the gods of Klakith were smiling on her today, Kris thought cheerfully. She glanced around, leaned forward, acting as if she was about to confide in the girl, then backed off. "Is there any coffee?" Kris asked.

Lyanne's eyes brightened with understanding. She mouthed an answer to Kris's unasked query. "He's in the office." Her lips formed the words with exaggerated care. "There's even fresh strawberries, French toast, and three kinds of syrup," Lyanne offered out loud. "Come on out to the kitchen."

Although breakfast was one meal that Kris had avoided for years, she decided it was more politic to eat. Once past the kitchen door, the smell of fresh coffee and the hint of maple syrup in the air reminded her that she'd barely touched her dinner the night before.

Once she was settled at the oak table with a steaming mug of black coffee, Kris picked up the thread of conversation. "What kind of band does Dean have? How many pieces? Do they play rock, country, polkas?"

Lyanne giggled. With a few deft moves, she had a fresh batch of French toast cooking on the griddle. "Definitely not polkas, although I think Mrs. Taggart would like it better if they did. Imagine! She wanted Dean to play an accordion instead of an electric guitar!"

Kris sipped her coffee. Not bad, but definitely not her usual imported blend. "Who knows? Maybe rap accordion music would be the unique ingredient that landed a recording contract."

"Rap accordion?" Lyanne twittered like a perky little robin at the mere idea. Then she sobered quickly. "Do you really think so? It could get a recording company interested in them?"

Kris hid her nose in her mug rather than face that sincere young face. "I was kidding, really. Does Dean's band play rap, then?"

"Not very well," Lyanne admitted. "But Dean says they

can't get the hang of it because none of them are from the big city."

Having no other answer to that one, Kris just nodded sagely, giving Lyanne the impression that she was very impressed with Dean's thought processes.

"They do a really great version of the old Rolling Stones' song, 'Satisfaction,' " the teenager volunteered.

Kris took the next step. "I'd like to hear them sometime. Will they be playing professionally anywhere while I'm here?"

Lyanne flipped the French toast over and turned to the refrigerator. "You mean like tonight?"

It was Saturday. There was a very good chance that a local group would be playing at a small club or a church- or school-related event.

Lyanne poured out a large glass of chocolate milk and sat it on the table. Kris was relieved to note it was not next to her plate. She turned down the offer of orange juice and accepted more coffee.

"They'll be practicing tonight, but that's not the same as playing a gig, is it?" the girl asked.

"Not quite," Kris allowed. "At least, it wasn't when Dead Heat had a practice session."

Lyanne was quite happy to hear more about Kris's tour with the popular band. Her eyes took on a dreamy quality. Quite often she sighed in sheer pleasure at some quirk of Tasker Fane's or that of another member of the band.

Kris found some aspects of her time with Dead Heat were actually amusing when related. It wasn't as if any of the long-haired musicians had possessed a sense of humor. But the fans who flocked to their performances had created bizarre situations. Of course, they hadn't been funny at the time. Kris had felt the distinct desire to strangle a few of the crafty little girls. But in retrospect, those same hassles actually sounded cute.

* * *

" . . . then in Minneapolis we got stuck in the hotel elevator," Kris said, nibbling on a plump strawberry. "There was this sound on the roof and a trapdoor was pulled open. Everyone thought it was a rescue party. Fane thought the cavalry had arrived."

Lyanne's glazed eyes blinked. "The what?"

"Cavalry. Like in the old westerns."

"Oh. John Wayne."

"Ah, yeah," Kris said after a moment. "The guys who wear blue uniforms and ride horses and shoot Indians."

Lyanne gave it her consideration, then nodded. "If you say so," she allowed. "What happened then?"

"Then?" Kris had lost her train of thought. "Ah . . ."

"In the stuck elevator with Tasker Fane," Lyanne prompted.

Kris finished her strawberry and buried her nose in her coffee cup. "So, the trapdoor opens and . . ."

"It's not the guys in blue uniforms."

"Right," Kris said. "Mostly because the horses wouldn't fit in the elevator shaft."

Lyanne giggled. "Who was it?"

"A couple of groupies. I thought for sure the extra weight would send us hurtling to the basement."

"But it didn't," Lyanne pointed out. "So what did the girls want?"

Kris thought quickly, deciding that the safest answer was the one Lyanne would think of herself. "Autographs."

"And Tasker and the others signed them eagerly," the girl declared, pleased at the outcome of the story.

Kris had no intention of mentioning how eager the young men had been to sign their names. Or on what part of the groupies' anatomy. Her own presence had put a stop to a more enthusiastic reception. When the elevator was once again in motion, she'd been the first one out when it hit the lobby.

Lyanne wasn't interested in how long the elevator had been stalled, compliments of Dead Heat's fans. The story ended happily once the autographs were given. Instead her mind had jumped ahead to Kris's current assignment.

"Is that what a tour with Roidan Ryder would be like?" the girl asked, her eyes very serious.

Since Kris couldn't picture fans of the Klakith novels being as rabid as teenaged groupies, she shook her head. "I doubt it. Much quieter."

Lyanne took a final gulp of milk and pushed her empty plate away. Kris was surprised to find she'd polished off her own helping of French toast and every strawberry in sight. When her young hostess waved the coffeepot, Kris took another refill.

"Well," Lyanne said, "the Klakith tour will be just you and Roidan Ryder, won't it?"

Kris had no intention of telling anyone that she was bowing out of the assignment once she got hold of Ryder. "Maybe. Maybe not."

"And what would you do if you were trapped in an elevator with him?"

This really was fantasy time, Kris thought. "Well, that's hard to say. What's he look like? Yoda?"

Lyanne giggled. She hadn't developed a variety of nuances yet. When amused, there was only the one lighthearted response. "Roidan doesn't look like Yoda," she said.

"You relieve my mind," Kris said.

"What if he looked like my brother Adam?"

"Same thing I'd do if I was with Yoda," Kris assured her. "Just wait patiently for rescue."

Lyanne wasn't happy with that answer. "Wouldn't you

be tempted to kiss him?" she persisted.

"No," Kris insisted quickly and, she hoped, authoritatively.

The teenager considered the short answer for a moment. "Is it because you're married?"

Kris gave a short burst of laughter. "I'm not married. Much to my mother's chagrin," she said.

"Engaged?"

"No, not . . ."

"Seeing someone?"

"I'm not home long enough usually to . . ."

"But you wouldn't want to kiss Adam?"

Kris found herself blushing. "I wouldn't be the only one involved, you know. It isn't just a matter of a woman wanting to be kissed but . . ."

"So if Adam wanted to kiss you, it would be okay?"

Lord above! What next? "I don't know. But since the situation will never arise . . ."

"You mean the elevator getting stuck." Lyanne nodded, her expression still deadly serious.

"Or being on tour with your brother," Kris added quickly. "There's no reason for him to accompany Ryder, after all. He can stay here and get the place ready for the summer vacationers."

"He never does that," Lyanne said. "Luther B. takes care of the lodge in the summer. We usually go someplace else for awhile. Last year it was Mexico."

Kris pushed her coffee cup aside. She would probably slosh when she walked, she'd had so many cups already. "So Roidan Ryder is alone up here during the tourist season?"

Lyanne stood up and began clearing the table. "Of course not," she said. "Adam is Roidan Ryder."

nine

IN THE LIVING ROOM AEROSMITH PLAYED ON AT A MUTED volume. The lead singer's insistent shout that the "Dude Looks Like a Lady" reached Adam at his desk. Unconsciously, Cheney sang along. He did like Aerosmith. Well, some of Aerosmith's stuff, at any rate. They'd been around long enough to almost count grandmothers in their audience. At least they were better, in his opinion, than Ozzy Osbourne or Metallica, two of Lyanne's other favorites.

The monitor was glowing. He'd tried to return to work after his sister dragged her current idol off to breakfast. Adam couldn't say he'd actually accomplished anything in the way of editing. There was too much on his mind to distract him from Dalwulf's final adventure.

The publisher wasn't pleased with his determination to end the Klakith series. They'd even pleaded. If he felt the Dealer himself had evolved to a point where his conscience would no longer allow him to run the bride trade, then why not move the setting a generation forward and let his son have a series of adventures, they had asked.

But Adam was sick of Klakith. Nearly two years ago he'd planned this final tale, planned to introduce a woman who would change Dalwulf's life. Emling. At the end of this last story the Dealer would be a happily married man. And Adam Cheney would begin writing stories himself. Roidan Ryder would stay with Dalwulf. In the archives.

From behind the closed kitchen door, he could hear Lyanne's excited babble, interspersed with Kris's soft, well-modulated tones, but he couldn't hear what was being said. He was pleased that their visitor had taken the first step toward winning Lyanne's trust without his having to beg her to do so. He suspected her motives, but then he had his own reasons for wanting a friendship to develop between the two.

Adam looked back at the screen, at the insistent blink of the cursor.

High above, the bloodred sandstone stretched fingers toward its father sun. Dalwulf stared at the spires. At the blushing sky. At anything but the woman who cowered, exhausted, at his feet.

In his mind's eye Adam pictured the steeply rising canyons of Zion National Monument, an hour's drive away. The first time he'd seen it, this whole corner of southwestern Utah had looked like the Middle World region of Klakith to him. When he was stumped for material, it only took a walk among the cliffs of Zion, or Bryce Canyon, to refuel his imagination.

He tapped thoughtfully at the stiff cast on his leg. It would still be weeks before he could hike the trails in comfort. The cast would be off in two days' time. But the rehabilitation of muscles and tendons would take longer. Especially with his knee.

Perhaps he had been lucky, as the doctor claimed. The break had been clean and the knee only twisted in his fall.

A stupid fall. But then he'd been temporarily insane to even attempt the advanced slope at Brianhead. So he'd fallen and broken his leg while trying to impress a stranger in a form fitting ski outfit. She hadn't even stayed interested long enough to sign his cast.

Lyanne had been contrite, blaming herself for requesting a long ski weekend to celebrate their birthdays, her sixteenth and his thirtieth. The dates fell within a week of each other and in between had been the four days of the Thanksgiving weekend.

The request had sounded like fun. Well, until he'd been stupid enough to break his leg, it had been fun. He did miss the ability to pace, to hike, to work out his frustrations through vigorous exercise.

Adam flexed his stiff shoulders and decided that even movement with the aid of his crutches was better than sitting still. A trip down to the dock and back was about all he could manage. It wasn't the distance, it was the irritation of moving slowly, of having the rubber tips of each crutch sink into the mud or slide on a patch of ice. He'd felt a total fool lying stretched out helpless and in pain on the ski run. Falling in the slush of early spring in his own front yard would be a worse humiliation.

Especially with Kris Jackson in residence to see him.

But he was too antsy to sit still any longer. He had to be on the move, out in the cool, brisk air. The weather report had called for a chance of showers. Or a final snow flurry. The clouds gave every promise of coming through, of backing up the meteorologist with a vengeance. If he wanted to get out, it was now or be holed up for days waiting for the weather to clear.

Swinging his crutches into place, Adam hobbled from his office.

Kris was still staring at her hostess in irritation when the back door flew open and a burly stranger thumped into the warm kitchen.

"Hi, Luther B.," Lyanne greeted, barely turning her head to nod at the man. "Coffee's on the stove."

"Hmmph," he said.

"This is Ms. Jackson," the girl added. "Luther B. Young. He helps out around here."

The man was on the wrong side of fifty, but the grizzled gray bristle of his beard could have been deceptive. A bright purple muffler was draped around his neck. His heavy jacket hung open. Beneath it Luther B. wore a flannel shirt in a red-and-black plaid. It was buttoned nearly to his throat. A touch of white thermal underwear showed near the collar. Luther B.'s trousers were stuffed into rubber boots, and a knit hat of kelly green was pulled down over his ears. His flaring thick brows were as speckled with gray as was his scruffy beard.

Kris said, "Pleased to meet you," in a voice that sounded far from pleased.

Luther B. busied himself with the coffee.

"Guess what the B stands for," Lyanne urged Kris. Her honey-golden eyes twinkled as she turned back to give Luther B. a wide grin.

"Bob?" Kris suggested. "Bruce? Brian?" Beelzebub, she thought, staring at those eyebrows again.

Lyanne giggled. "Brigham!" she crowed.

Luther B. shrugged. "It's Utah," he grumbled. "Can't help gettin' old Brigham's moniker if you're a Young."

Kris didn't know if she should congratulate or sympathize with him.

"Luther B. is a Mormon," Lyanne confided. "But not a very good one. He's not supposed to drink caffeine, but he does. We aren't Mormons. Neither is Dean. But my best friend Becky is. I've gone to some of the craft meetings at her church. Her mother claims every Mormon woman is an expert with a glue gun 'cause they do so many homemaking projects."

"Oh," Kris said, at a loss as to how to respond.

"Don't have more'n one wife now neither," Luther B. added, with an evil smile. "More's the pity."

The pity for whom? Kris didn't envy any woman who looked after Luther B. one bit. "Ah . . . yes." Kris turned back to Lyanne. "What did you say about Roidan Ryder?"

Lyanne giggled. "You didn't believe me? It's true. Ask Luther B." Without giving Kris a chance, the girl twisted in her chair. "Tell Ms. Jackson who Roidan really is," she urged.

The man's nose was buried in his coffee cup. Possibly to warm it. "Adam," he said shortly. "Who else is there?"

Kris would have been more willing to accept that Luther B. himself was Roidan Ryder. "Cheney can't be," she said.

Lyanne's eyes widened in interest. "Why not?"

"Well . . . he's . . . he's . . ."

"He's Dalwulf," Lyanne said. "Or sorta. Adam used to tell me the stories before I went to bed. They were always better than the fairy tales or books that other kids had because he'd ask me what kind of story I wanted first. Then he'd invent it."

Kris's look was very skeptical. "I don't think your mother would have cared for you to hear stories about a man who sold women."

"Wulfy doesn't do that," Lyanne declared. "Besides, Mommy and Daddy were . . . gone then. It was just Adam and me, so we could have any kind of story we wanted. I liked Klakith because it was so different from home."

Luther B. grunted. "It's different, all right. You gonna give your pinto a run? Taggart's boy is already down at the barn with the bay. Wants to know if you're coming or not."

"I'm on my way," the girl insisted. "Just make yourself at home, Ms. Jackson. If there's anything you want, help yourself." Then she was out the door, pulling on her pale ski jacket as she went. Luther B. trailed behind.

Alone in the kitchen, Kris stared blankly at her coffee mug. Either everyone was in on the cover-up or she had to accept it as fact, she supposed. But there was something inside her that rebelled at the idea of Roidan Ryder and Adam Cheney being one and the same. She really needed more viable proof. Not just verbal identifications. But what kind? And how did she get it? Sneak up behind Cheney and call him Ryder to see if he answered? Of course he'd answer. It was part of the plan.

Maybe there would be more hints in the Klakith tales. She'd read last night until three in the morning, when exhaustion made it possible to sleep on the hard floor. The cabin was a slight bit warmer but not enough to merit returning to it just yet. The lodge was much too cozy.

Kris looked around the kitchen. It was far from barbaric. A large double-door refrigerator and a multitude of cupboards housed a more-than-ample supply of food. The stove top had a separate griddle, and twin ovens were located on the wall. There was a dishwasher, trash compactor, microwave, and even a bread-making machine! The wide window over the sink looked out over a vista of woodland and snow-covered meadowland. Further exploration showed the back door led to a long, enclosed porch with still more supplies. Large bushel baskets of paper-wrapped apples and pears sat on metal shelves. Another of potatoes was near the door. Bouquets of spices hung from the low rafters. There was even a fifty-pound bag of dogfood for the Irish setter and numerous cases of cola. The room wasn't as warm as the cozy kitchen, but it was heated sufficiently to keep the supplies from freezing at night.

Nor was it warm enough to tempt Kris to explore it in depth. She closed the door softly and moved across the kitchen, her steps hushed. She didn't feel like a showdown this early with Adam. For that's what every conversation with him had been. He had been the winner the night before, leaving her muddled with that declaration of a dual identity. With Lyanne and Luther B. backing up the idea that Adam was Roidan Ryder, she still wasn't thinking straight. So it was back to the Klakith books for her. She'd made it through yet another whole story last night and, in spite of her better self, found she liked Dalwulf. Or Wulfy, as Lyanne called him. Too bad she couldn't say the same about his double, Adam Cheney.

The stereo system was still working its way from one side of the Aerosmith tape to the other and back again. Apparently Cheney was not as averse to the group as his sister thought. He hadn't hobbled from his office and ripped the cassette from the tape player, at any rate.

Kris tiptoed out of the kitchen and crept nearer the open office door. If she could whisk past, she could be back in front of the Franklin stove freezing within minutes.

When she peeped, there was no one in the office, though. The steady pulse of the cursor on the computer screen showed that someone had been working earlier, and would soon return. If it were Cheney, she'd be warned by the thump of his crutches on the wooden flooring. If it were

the real Roidan Ryder, though, she hoped he caught her
snooping so she could put an end to the charade and finish
her assignment. Kris slid into the room.

It was small and crowded. Overcrowded. Three of the
walls were floor-to-ceiling shelves lined with books. The
chronicles of Klakith didn't rest here, though. She read
through the titles, noting that the same authors were
repeated numerous times. They weren't all science fiction.
A good number were mysteries. Isaac Asimov sat next to
Ross MacDonald. All of Anne McCaffrey's dragon riders
of Pern adventures were grouped together. Terry Brooks,
the boy wonder Adam had mentioned, had a number of
thick volumes all dealing with adventures of Shannara.
Ace, DAW, Tor, Del Rey, and TSR publications showed
thorough and frequent readings. But so did Tony Hillerman's
mysteries and Gregory Macdonald's Fletch series. Kris went
down the row, shelf by shelf. Robin Cook, Dean Koontz,
Umberto Eco, Marion Zimmer Bradley, Andre Norton,
Robert Ludlum, Charlotte MacLeod, and Donald Westlake
all rubbed shoulders.

Although the area was small, it was compactly arranged.
The desk faced out into the room allowing space for a small
copier and facsimile machine. An electric typewriter was
pushed aside, replaced by the IBM personal computer on
the desk. A laser printer, squeezed into the space between
the desk and window, sat on an old-fashioned metal typewriter table.

A view of the lake could be enjoyed from an overstuffed,
tweed-upholstered reclining chair. Arranged so that it made
ample use of the light from the window or from the floor
lamp, the chair had the air of a favorite retreat. On the
narrow table next to it was a stack of magazines. All
were recent issues of *Publishers Weekly*. If this was Adam
Cheney's office, Kris would have expected to see fishing

digests. It just seemed to prove that Roidan Ryder and Cheney were indeed two different men rather than one.

She worked her way around to the desk and sat down in the plush swivel chair. On the computer screen was the text of a Klakith novel. Kris ignored it for the time being, intent on finding physical evidence that would lead her to Roidan Ryder.

There was a stack of deep baskets on the desk corner. The top was marked "In," the lower "Out." The bottom was filled nearly to overflowing. Either Lyanne was behind on the filing or Ryder let everything pile up awaiting Cheney's attention. Since Adam had been on crutches for some time now, he'd probably slacked off on his work schedule. It was perfect for Kris's purpose, though. She rifled through the papers quickly.

Asteroid Books' logo was at the top of a number of sheets. They were arguing about a change in Ryder's output. Something about his retiring, and how could they trust the quality of material that he promised this Cheney guy could write?

So Adam Cheney thought he could write fantasy novels, too. Kris chewed her lip as she digested the information.

Ryder had followed with a fresh declaration of faith in the abilities of his agent, signing the letter with a hasty fluency. Kris noted the flamboyant capital letters followed by tightly grouped, stilted script. She wasn't one to put much faith in handwriting analysis, but it was an easy bet that his signature showed a man who was self-controlled and itching to break loose. Those sweeping R's had to mean the creator of Klakith would enjoy getting away from this mountain retreat and out into the real world on a publicity tour.

She leafed through another inch. A Xerox of the proof edited copy of the nineteenth book was there. It showed the corrections made by an editor and those Ryder had made since turning in the final manuscript. Adam claimed to proof all the stories, but obviously Ryder didn't leave everything in his agent's hands.

Kris hesitated. This was the first story in which Emling, her twin with the blue skin, appeared. Would anyone notice if she swiped it? They would if it were gone long. Best to leave it in the basket and lift it later after she'd worked her way through the series.

She dug further, finding letters from Cheney himself in the batch. They were answers to requests from various avid fishermen for reservations at Klakith Lodge. Apparently the summer would swell the population at the lake a great deal. Not only were the log cabins scheduled to be filled, but a number of campsites had been reserved as well.

Kris started to push them back into the pile, far from interested in the life cycle of the lodge. Then she stopped, stunned at the proof evident in the letters.

Anxiously, she thumbed back through the stack of filing until she had a number of other letters to use as a comparison. She laid them out on the desk, the signatures nearly touching.

Swooping, grandstand capitals and constricted, closely grouped lower-case letters. Although both autographs were different names, the hand that had written them was the same.

No one had tried to con her. Adam Cheney *was* Roidan Ryder!

Kris sat staring at the letters. Slowly, disbelief gave way to conviction, and then to fury. How dare he string her along! He should have admitted to being Ryder when she first accosted him at the dock! He should have told the people back in New York that he worked under the pseudonym Roidan Ryder. But judging from what she'd read in the correspondence between Asteroid Books and "Ryder," Adam was pretending to be his own mentor. The nerve of the man! He'd set everything up so that when he did confess, no one would believe him anyway. A manipulator, that's what Adam Cheney was.

Well, she wouldn't stay. She'd go back to civilization and she'd blow his cozy little setup. She'd tell Asteroid's editors that Ryder was as much a figment of their imaginations as Dalwulf the Dealer was. That Adam had been playing them for fools for years.

And making money at it!

Boiling mad, Kris shoved the damning letters back into the basket, no longer anxious to cover her spying activities. She was going to find Adam Cheney, blister his ears good with a full telling of her low opinion of him and what she planned to do to destroy his credibility back in New York City. Then she'd get in her rented BMW and drive back down to civilization.

Almost blind with fury, Kris stormed out of the office and smack into Adam Cheney.

ten

HE WAS STILL DRESSED FOR THE COLD, HIS HEAVY JACKET hanging open, his single Reebok slightly damp. He had put the crutches aside to struggle out of his coat and was balancing on his uninjured leg.

Or at least he was until Kris's angry rush knocked her into him.

One arm still tangled in his coat sleeve, Adam went down like a felled redwood.

"Oh, damn!" Kris gasped. In reflex, she grabbed at him and found herself flat on the floor with him.

Adam's eyes were closed tightly, his teeth gritted in pain. He took a ragged breath.

Contrite, Kris touched his cheek gently. "Are you all right?"

"In a minute." His voice was raw but when Adam opened his eyes, Kris could see that the shadow of pain was already beginning to fade from their golden depths.

A strange deep gold, like molten lava. In fact, the look in his eyes had the same effect as a lava flow because, wherever his gaze caressed her, Kris seemed to burn. The touch of his hands on her arms was just as fevered.

Her breath came in quick gasps, making the soft wool of her sweater rise and fall alluringly. Somehow they'd twisted, entangling limbs as they fell. Although the heavy cast had hit the floor with a resounding crash, Adam now lay partially on top of her, as if he'd bounced, his good leg resting intimately between her thighs.

She worried a bit about how his broken leg had reacted to the fall. But that was the only part of his anatomy that might have suffered. There was another part of him that was definitely all right. It wasn't the stiffness of plaster and gauze that pressed against her as they lay entwined. She squirmed to heave him aside.

Despite the sharp pain that had now begun to ebb, Adam grinned down into her face. "You're only making it worse," he pointed out in amusement.

Kris's coloring rose. It wasn't just Adam's body that was responding to the closeness of their prone position. Her own was acting very strangely. Far too warm and alive.

"Get the hell off me, Cheney," she spat.

"I'd be glad to oblige if I could." He did roll over, albeit reluctantly, disentangling their limbs.

Kris scrambled to her feet. "I've got a bone to pick with you," she hissed.

Adam sighed, still lying at her feet. Rather, he thought, in the same position that he'd just left Emling reclining before Dalwulf. "A new one? Or merely re-gnawing a tasty old one? Find fault with your suite?"

"Stand up," Kris snapped. "I can't talk to you while you're lying down."

A rather fiendish grin lit those disturbing eyes and crinkled their corners. "You could join me," he offered.

"Get the hell up, Cheney. I'm in no mood to play games."

"And I'm in no shape to obey your summons, slick," he countered. "You might have noticed I'm not exactly unencumbered. In fact, I feel like a blasted turtle, stranded on my back."

Kris sneered down at him.

Adam wished she'd worn the form-fitting thigh-high boots again, then decided he was better off seeing Kris Jackson's deliciously long legs disguised in the fuller-cut gray slacks today.

"A turtle?" she said. "I would have thought a wood roach was more your speed."

"I think I prefer the turtle simile. You'll have to help me up," Adam pointed out. "Unless you feel like curling up down here again. We could have quite a cozy conversation while waiting for Luther B. or Dean to come to the rescue."

Kris looked at the ceiling in resignation. "Lord help us," she murmured in disgust. "Okay, what do I have to do? Just tug on your hand?"

"You could yank on whatever part you want, slick, but it won't get me back on my feet. If that's your goal, that is."

She gritted her teeth at him and nearly growled in frustration. He was enjoying this far too much. Those damn wolf eyes were still dancing with amusement.

"What would you do if I wasn't here?"

"Well, for one thing, I would have avoided falling down," he said.

Kris showed more teeth. "Let's say you managed it anyway because you're a clumsy oaf," she suggested.

Adam rubbed his chin in thought. "Probably scoot over

to the staircase and work my way up, one step at a time, till I could use the banister to pull myself upright," he admitted.

"And you couldn't do that without my help?"

"It could take hours."

Kris snorted. "You don't look that puny. But I suppose I could help. What do you want me to do? Drag you over there?"

"Like a husky sled dog in harness? I'd probably be back in traction if you tried. How about if you just bring the crutches over?"

"I can handle that."

"It didn't seem beyond your capabilities," Adam said. "Just refrain from turning them into cattle prods in your impatience."

Kris gathered the crutches while Adam propelled himself, a few inches at a time, back toward the staircase. Kris strode up the first few treads and made herself comfortable halfway up. He made the trip in much less time than she would have thought possible and was soon sitting next to her, the cast stretched out, his good leg bent in a companionable stance. He leaned an elbow on his upraised knee and studied her a moment.

"Nope," Adam said at last. "That's wrong. Your cheekbones are too high."

New thunderclouds gathered in her blue eyes. Her brows knitted over the bridge of her nose. "Too high for what?"

"For you to be Emling, of course. I thought you'd take that as a compliment, slick."

He was laughing at her again. Damn the man.

"So what did you want to berate me about this time?" Adam asked.

Somehow his question took the wind out of her sails. Kris drew a deep breath. Her voice was calm rather than furious when she spoke. "Why didn't you tell me you were Roidan Ryder?"

Adam's brows rose in surprise. They were like slashes. Dark, red . . . no, rusty . . . very rusty slashes. Not like normal eyebrows. They nearly disappeared beneath the tumbled forelock of hair that fell over his forehead. He looked unruly, windswept, and he smelled of fresh air, pine trees, and bay rum aftershave.

"I did tell you I was Ryder," he said. "Last night. I was under the impression that you heard. But, of course, I'm basing that on the way you left in a huff."

So much for a civilized discussion. Kris's temper engaged once more. "I did not leave in a huff!"

"Quibbling about my word choice, huh?" Adam leaned back, elbows on the step behind him. "Not picturesque enough? Let's see. I suppose I could do better."

"Don't bother straining yourself."

Adam grinned wickedly at her. "Oh, no trouble. Trust me, slick, you'll know when I'm straining myself over you."

Kris glared. "Are these sophomoric innuendos supposed to impress me or scare me away?"

He seemed to give the question a bit of thought. "I suppose," he admitted at length, "that it depends on the number of tequila shots you've tossed off."

Kris felt a distinct urge to strangle him. But that wouldn't work. She'd have to touch him to accomplish that feat. Unfortunately, while lying on the floor in his arms, she'd experienced a distinctly nonviolent reaction to Adam Cheney's touch.

"Lord, you're a disgusting creep," she said. "Why didn't you tell me when I asked yesterday at the dock?"

He had the nerve to chuckle. "Principles. Camouflage. Peace of mind. Take your pick."

"General orneriness, I'd believe."

"You're the first person to whom I've ever blatantly confessed," he said.

Kris gave him a look of contempt. "That's supposed to smooth over everything? Heal all wounds?"

"Do you have wounds, slick? I'm willing to kiss them well."

"You have a pathetically one-track mind," she insisted.

"Can't help it. If you hadn't knocked me down and squirmed all over me . . ."

Her growl was very distinct now. Adam was pleased to note that Kris didn't make a motion to leave, though. Perhaps he wasn't the only one whose mind stubbornly dwelt on those few moments of intimacy.

"So what are we going to do about it?" she asked.

The question took him by surprise. "Well," he drawled, his voice pitched to a throbbing, deep purr, "we could continue up the stairs, bar the door and continue where we left off down there on the parquet."

"You have delusions of grandeur," Kris answered. "That is not parquet flooring. Just a series of slapped-down boards."

She hadn't actually refused his flippant, and far from serious suggestion, Adam realized. Had she seen it as just a glib remark, as he'd meant it? Could Kris Jackson actually see through him that easily? Had she second-guessed him, known that he'd never make love to her under his own roof? Not while there was the distinct possibility that his sister would walk in and catch them?

"Let's cut the crap, shall we?" Kris requested. "There's this damn movie to promote and numerous volumes of Klakith novels to be autographed. Are you going on the publicity tour?"

Adam leaned forward and absently massaged the small

section of thigh above his cast. "It would blow my cover to do it."

"Your cover? Hell, this isn't a Le Carre spy story, Cheney. It's just a promotion tour. A few whistle-stops to shake hands, smile for photographers, and be pawed by fans. You'll probably enjoy that last bit particularly."

He stared ahead. "I can't leave Lyanne. She's just a kid, you know."

"Okay." Kris nodded in agreement. "I can understand that. She's at a dangerous age to be left on her own. Especially when she's got a boyfriend."

"Amen to that. Unless . . ." He paused and turned to study Kris.

She squirmed under his look. It wasn't suggestive or caressing now. It measured her for something that didn't include a bed this time.

"Unless what?"

"Unless you're willing to tame her."

Kris blinked. "*Tame* your sister? Like she was a lion or something?"

"Yyyeeaahhh." He drew the word out lazily. "You could do it, slick. She admires you. Cut her loose from her fascination with Dean Taggart. Make her settle back into childhood rather than rush into being an adult."

Kris was sure she hadn't heard right. "You're kidding."

"Nope. Dead serious."

"And if I agree, and fail?"

Adam spread his hands as if admitting defeat. "Well, then I can't do the tour, can I? My first loyalty is to taking care of my little sister. Klakith has been taking care of itself for years. It won't miss me."

Kris chewed on her lip in thought. "Not even when you finish the chronicles and kill off Roidan Ryder?"

"They told you he was planning to retire, did they?"

She had no intention of admitting she'd only learned of it from ferreting through the correspondence on his desk.

Adam smirked, his lips twisting sarcastically. "Time to move on, slick. Is it a deal, then?"

Kris stared at him, still chewing thoughtfully at her lip.

When Adam's eyes dropped to her mouth, his expression softening, she sat up straighter and took a deep breath. Tame a teenager? She remembered how anxious she'd been to escape the confines of childhood at the same age. Remembered her first love, a preppy jock with a wide smile and fast hands.

He'd had nice hair, too. Not as rich as Adam Cheney's dark red-tinged locks. Nor as long. Rather than follow the current trend to either shear his hair short or pull it back into a ponytail, Adam clung to an older style. Although shaped, his hair curled almost to his shoulders. It was quite a bit longer than her own cropped hairdo. Something about it—the length?—the color?—made Kris want to bury her fingers in those thick waves.

"Should we make this deal in writing?" she asked.

"Too formal," Adam said. His eyes had taken on that amused twinkle that infuriated her. His tone was flippant once more. "There are other, more pleasant ways to seal it."

Kris frowned at him. "I think a handshake would be sufficient. You wouldn't want to give Lyanne any ideas should she happen to walk in."

"No, I suppose not." He sounded very disappointed but those golden glints belied the act. "Let's lay out the details, shall we?"

She hated him. Adam was too damn cheerful about this deal. Was it because he knew she would fail and thus relieve him of the necessity of going on tour? Or was it merely that he saw it all as a play to be put on for his private amusement? Kris almost believed the latter.

"I get Lyanne to dump Dean and not look for a replacement boyfriend, and you go on the road for Klakith," she said.

Adam squinted one eye. One side of his mouth curved up. "Not exactly, slick. True, I could do without a steady boyfriend hanging around. I prefer that she do things like school dances as part of a large group, not on a one-to-one basis with the opposite sex. We're too hungry a breed."

"That I'll buy," Kris admitted, having just received a very predatory glance along with the lecture.

"Next, I want her taste in clothing modified. Right now Lye's skirts are too short, too tight, too damn suggestive. And those off-the-shoulder blouses and body suits . . . ?"

"I get the picture," Kris growled. "You've got one hell of a double standard, don't you?"

"Damn right. What man hasn't? If she wants to give you all her discarded clothes, it's fine with me. But I'd want a private fashion show."

"Oh, go to hell, Cheney."

He laughed at the recommendation. "And another thing," he said. "When you go on a shopping spree with Lye, don't let her get any of those wading boots like yours."

"Don't like them?"

"Slick, you are a naive little beauty, aren't you?"

Kris's eyes widened. No one had ever considered her *little* before. The idea made her a bit dizzy. "What's wrong with my boots?"

Adam pulled himself upright and reached for his crutches. "Nothing that ice-cold showers can't cure," he assured her. "Be gentle with me, would you?"

Kris surged to her feet in fury. "Gentle! You . . . you *klindtz!*"

It was Adam's turn to be surprised. She'd just insulted

him with a Klakith expletive. Not one of the nicer ones, either. He chuckled in delight.

The sound of his amusement pushed Kris over the edge. She swung at him, but Adam dodged the blow. The movement made him wobble anew. Instantly contrite, Kris grabbed for him to prevent a second fall, this time down the stairs.

For a moment they were frozen in place. Kris's hands on his biceps. She stared into his wonderfully dramatic feral eyes. Watched them swirl with emotion. Mesmerized, her hands slid up his arms and around Adam's neck.

Adam dropped his crutches. Kris barely heard the sound as they hit the floor. She was conscious only of the feel of him beneath her hands, of his hands as they encompassed her waist and pulled her nearer.

Caught in a spell neither had sought, Kris tipped her lips up to his as Adam's mouth dipped toward hers.

eleven

THEY WERE A SCANT BREATH APART WHEN THE FRONT door swung open and Dean Taggart stomped in.

Kris and Adam sprang apart guiltily.

"Morning, Ms. Jackson," Dean said, then turned his attention to Lyanne's brother. "Lye and I are riding the horses up around the far end of the lake," he explained, either purposefully blind to the intimate scene he'd interrupted, or incredibly dense. "Do you want us to check anything out? Snow's melting pretty fast now."

Without being asked, Dean picked up the forgotten crutches and handed them to Adam.

"You might look over the campgrounds at that end," Cheney said, his voice much calmer than Kris felt. "Looks like we'll be booked solid," he added, and hobbled back down the stairs.

Dean nodded. "We'll be back in time for lunch then." He was gone as quickly as he'd come. This time, they heard the clump of his boots on the porch after the door swung shut.

Kris looked down at Adam, balancing on his crutches once more at the bottom of the staircase. "I'd better start planning my campaign," she said. "If we expect to meet the schedule of appearances, I don't have much time to convert your sister."

"I suppose not," he agreed.

"I'll . . . ah . . . go to my cabin and wait for her to come back," she suggested. Her footsteps lagged, though.

Kris was almost to the door when Adam spoke. "Isn't there something you've forgotten to ask?" he murmured.

She doubted if coherent thought was possible yet. Her body still burned from his touch. Her mind still rebelled at the weakness displayed by her body.

At her blank look, Adam took pity on her. "The cast comes off Monday," he said.

Kris wondered if that simple statement wasn't more of a warning. He'd be unencumbered on the tour. But he'd also be far too vital in the coming days as well. Somehow the look in those molten eyes didn't promise anything remotely like a cold shower.

Lyanne settled her body into the stride of her pinto. She led the way, cantering around the lake. Her mount's breath came back in a stream of visible vapor. The air was crisp but she could discern a warming in the weather. Spring was definitely nearby. The thought of warmer days made her tingle with excitement, because the change in seasons signaled that school would soon be out and she could spend even more time with Dean.

"Look! There are the cardinals!" she shouted back to him. She pulled on the reins to slow her horse to a walk, stood in her stirrups, and pointed.

Dean drew Adam's big bay up beside her. "What are they doing? House hunting?"

The birds flitted from tree to tree. As soon as one landed, the other followed, only to be left alone as the female played the coquette and the male pandered to her flirtatious mood.

"Probably not," Lyanne admitted. "They always seem to nest in the same area. I'm still amazed that they come back every year."

"They just know paradise when they see it," Dean said.

Lyanne giggled. "Klakith Lodge? It's not exactly my idea of a lovers' paradise."

"You wouldn't think so if you'd been the one to go into the lodge to tell Adam where we were going," he hinted.

Her honey eyes widened. "You mean, he and Ms. Jackson . . ."

"Almost. I'm afraid I interrupted the mood. Although maybe not. They were on the stairs. And what else is on the second floor except for your bedrooms?"

"You think they're lovers already?" Lyanne sighed. "That's too much to hope for yet. But still . . . what were they doing?"

Dean laughed. "The same thing we do when we're alone, baby."

"Whoa! Kissing! Wait till I tell Becky!"

"Don't count your chickens, Lye," he warned.

She scoffed at him. "It's a totally awesome event, Dean. Do you know how long it has been since Adam's had a regular girlfriend?"

"Too long?"

"Years!" she insisted dramatically. "I can't remember him being really interested in anyone since Miss Leigh, my fourth-grade teacher. That was before we moved here!" Lyanne paused thoughtfully. "Of course I was glad when he stopped dating her. It was really weird wondering if my teacher was going to become my sister-in-law. She wanted me to call her Maggie on the weekends but I couldn't."

Dean nodded in agreement. He'd found that was easier than trying to follow Lyanne's agile mind as it moved swiftly from subject to subject.

" 'Course, I haven't gotten up nerve to call Ms. Jackson by her first name either," Lyanne admitted.

They reached the farthest campsite. Dean pulled his horse to a stop and dismounted. "I'm glad you never called me Mr. Taggart, then," he teased her.

"Maybe I should start," she suggested with a giggle, and slid out of the saddle into his arms.

Her pinto and Adam's bay stood quietly, their heads bent to nuzzle at the blades of grass that appeared through the melting snow.

"I'll make you a deal," Dean said huskily against Lyanne's neck. "You can call me Mr. Taggart when you're Mrs. Taggart."

She tilted her head back, allowing her long red-gold hair to fall over his hands on her back. She stared up into his face. "Or we could just pretend I'm Mrs. Taggart," she murmured softly.

Dean kissed her. Lyanne's mouth opened eagerly, welcoming the urgent thrust of his tongue along hers. He was panting when they parted.

"I thought you wanted to wait," he said.

"You mean to . . ." She left the sentence hanging and blushed. "I do. You didn't think I meant . . ."

"Yes, I did." He sounded hurt.

"But . . ."

Dean silenced her with another deep, desperate kiss. He needed to put space between them. It had been easy to make that decision last night. Harder to stop himself from driving back up to the lodge that morning.

"I talked to the guys," he said, still cuddling her close. "They want to try Vegas, too."

Lyanne's face suddenly looked years older. Nearly a match to the maturity of her figure. "When do you leave?"

"Not for awhile yet. We need to practice a bit more. Work out a couple more arrangements. Get in touch with a booking agent. Stuff like that."

"An agent?"

Dean felt he could almost see the light bulb go on over her pretty little head. Her expression was so easy to read.

"Ms. Jackson might know someone. She knows Tasker Fane and the rest of Dead Heat," she reminded.

"Yeah," Dean said. "But would she help us?"

Lyanne pressed close against him, her cotton-candy ski jacket nestled to his fatigue-green down-filled vest. "I'll ask her," she promised.

High above, the cardinals tired of their game and perched close together on a branch high above the young lovers.

Kris watched for Lyanne and her boyfriend to finish their inspection of the campground. From the vantage point of her cabin window she saw them first as specks on the far side of the lake. But as the tiny figures grew larger, she tried to throw the semblance of a plan together.

How was she supposed to pry Dean Taggart from Lyanne's side? She didn't know of anyone who would believe such a feat was possible. Other than Adam Cheney, that is.

He'd come up with the whole idea just to get her off his back over the publicity tour, of course. He expected her to fail. That was why he'd spelled out his terms in such mission-impossible detail. What he didn't know was that

Joel Halsey had trained her to be the perfect MI operator.

Hell, she'd seduce Dean herself if that's what it took. Well, maybe as a last resort. At the moment all she could think about was what might happen once Adam was free of his cast.

She still couldn't believe she'd come so close to kissing him. What was the matter with her? She was acting as man-hungry as her mother . . . Good grief! It couldn't be genetic, could it? That futile quest for the perfect love? It had taken Belinda in and out of marriage and a few nonsanctioned relationships as well. She never lost faith that she'd latch onto Mr. Right one of these days. In the meantime, Kris's mother seemed quite content to spend her time with a series of Mr. Almost-Rights.

Adam Cheney would definitely line up with that last category. For some perverse reason, nature had decided to give her an unreasonable physical attraction to the man. But it ended there. She'd make sure it ended there—before she succumbed to the lure of those insincere, lighthearted, suggestive quips.

Perhaps the best thing was to make sure they were never alone together. Kris was very sure that the tone of Adam's conversation would stay on the straight-and-narrow in his sister's presence.

Although she was determined to catch Lyanne before the girl returned to the main lodge, Kris was surprised when her young hostess dismounted in front of her own frozen little cabin and let Dean lead the pinto back toward the barn.

"I hope I'm not disturbing you," Lyanne apologized after tapping on the door.

"Not at all. Come in and become a Popsicle along with me," Kris greeted.

"You're still cold?"

"I'm thinking of joining a Polar Bear club," Kris said. "This is just training to toughen me up for those icy dips with the other members."

Lyanne giggled. She bent to check the Franklin stove's glowing stomach and found it full of wood. Flames licked eagerly at each piece. "I don't understand why it isn't working," she said and closed the cast-iron door.

Kris stared at the stove for a moment. "You closed the door," she said.

"Yeah." Lyanne shrugged out of her jacket. "So the heat doesn't escape. That way the whole thing heats up."

"You mean the door has to be closed for it to work?" Kris demanded, dumbfounded.

Lyanne grinned. Unfortunately Kris found that condescending amusement was much too much like the girl's older brother's smirk. "You didn't know that?"

"No. Who the hell invented it that way?"

The girl's giggle filled the cabin. "I think he was kinda famous," she said. "Ben Franklin."

"The guy with the kite, electricity, and the Declaration of Independence." Kris stared at the stove in loathing. The damn thing was working. She could already feel a difference in the cabin's temperature.

"Adam says it was the first effective central heating," Lyanne explained.

Kris didn't want to hear anymore about the girl's big brother. "I hope you came by to invite me to lunch."

"You don't need an invitation. You're our guest. But I did come here for a reason."

"It doesn't have anything to do with getting stuck in elevators again, does it?"

There was that giggle again. Maybe she should try to tame its frequency, Kris thought, then decided it would be impossible. Only people who weren't content with their lives held merriment back. She would be taking enough away from Lyanne if she succeeded in meeting Cheney's requirements. Let her keep the asinine giggle. Time would tame it to a more decorous sound.

"Actually, it's almost like that," Lyanne admitted.

Oh, Lord, Kris thought, and decided she needed to be sitting down for this. She offered her visitor the choice of a hard-backed chair or the nest of blankets near the stove. When Lyanne opted for the cozy pile on the floor, Kris plunked down next to her.

"When you were on tour with Dead Heat, did you meet any booking agents?" the girl asked.

Kris saw her opening. "For Dean's band, you mean?"

Lyanne nodded eagerly. "They'll never get anywhere here in Cedar City. They were thinking of trying Las Vegas."

"Hmm. Tough place to break in. I think they should try places like Tucson, Sacramento, maybe Santa Fe, before they attempt Vegas. There's too much competition there. Especially since so many of the shows went to taped music during the strike . . ."

"Oh, yeah. The musicians' strike," Lyanne said. "Dean told me about it."

"Of course those weren't rock-and-roll bands that were affected. Still . . ."

Lyanne wasn't about to be put off. But then Kris knew if she offered to help too soon, her prey might see the trap yawning before her. "Maybe if you heard them play you could tell if the group is any good?" Lyanne suggested.

"I'm no expert," Kris hedged.

"But you were with Dead Heat for three months!"

As if that qualified anyone, Kris thought. "I suppose I know a little," she admitted reluctantly.

Lyanne was ecstatic. "Maybe you could go to their practice tomorrow afternoon," she suggested. "That is, if you don't have anything else planned."

"Not a thing," Kris declared. "I'd love to go."

twelve

WHEN LYANNE LEFT THE TINY CABIN, SO DID KRIS. THE teenager nearly bounced with excitement as she headed back to the barn to tell Dean to prepare his band for visitors the following afternoon. Kris waited until Lyanne was halfway across the field before making a mad dash back to the main lodge.

Adam was in his office. He didn't seem to be working, just staring at the computer screen. Kris didn't bother knocking. She rushed in and swooped down on the phone on his desk.

"Start packing, Dealer," she snarled at him. Kris punched a New York number and perched on the edge of the desk, listening to the steady ring as she waited. "This is going to be as easy as . . ."

She broke off as a familiar voice answered the phone. The tone was groggy and irritable. Kris wasn't feeling charitable toward her mentor, though. "Halsey!" she shouted into the receiver. "You bastard! You set me up!"

Kris held the phone away from her ear as Joel Halsey tried to cover his mistake. She grinned superiorly at Adam. "My boss," she explained. "He has a hangover."

Adam leaned back in his chair. An excited babbling still issued from the phone. "And you're such a soothing person to minister to it. Personally, slick, I'd rather have a mule kick me in the head than have you fluttering around my sickbed."

On the other end of the connection, Halsey was still babbling. Kris chuckled. "So just how like Florence Nightingale is this Emling?"

"Emling?"

The squeak came from the phone, not Adam, Kris realized. She put the receiver to her ear. "Yes, Emling," she snarled. "You used me, Halsey. Me! Your so-called pride and joy! You've been lying to me all along."

Again she held the instrument away and let the man back in New York debase himself, unheard.

"I admire the way you called him collect," Adam said.

"But I didn't . . . oh, I see. Sarcasm. Well, you can afford the call. Your proposition didn't spell out use of utilities in detail. Besides, there's a method to my madness," Kris assured cockily.

The desk chair squeaked as Adam settled himself comfortably to watch her in action. It took moxie to be a success in her chosen profession. He'd known she was a feisty opponent, but seeing Kris in action against a different enemy was illuminating.

Halsey's whine was losing speed. Kris put the phone back to her ear, the receiver propped between her cheek and one hunched shoulder. She studied her nails. Brushed invisible lint from the knee of her dark slacks.

"You know," she purred, "Skip Sanderson offered me a vice presidency with his PR firm."

Halsey hissed loudly, like a cat.

"I don't care if he does want me horizontal on the top of a desk," Kris answered. "How did you intend that I deal with this Ryder character? Any differently?" she pushed. "You threw me in as an Emling look-alike, knowing exactly what Ryder would think was being offered."

Halsey protested.

Kris wasn't listening, though. "It wasn't a tour you were pushing, Halsey, but a whirlwind vacation with one of his own characters."

Halsey only got one word in this time before she continued.

"One stop at a time, from city to city, like some Earth equivalent of a Dalwulf escapade. A fantasy come true," Kris said.

Adam snorted. "My fantasies are better than that," he insisted.

Kris didn't bother to hold the phone away. She gave him a cheeky grin. "The written ones?"

Adam raised his voice loud enough to be heard by the man in New York as well. "The private ones."

She chuckled. "You hear that, Halsey? The man's dreaming up scenarios that would make Skip Sanderson weak in the knees."

"Better believe it," Adam murmured, but in a much quieter, and intimate tone.

"Whoa, boy," Kris said. "Lord, Halsey, you don't know what I'm up against here. Talk about your rabid Klakithites!" Her grin widened.

Halsey was babbling again.

"Of course Ryder's here," Kris purred. "I'm nearly in his lap."

"In two more days, it's all yours, slick," Adam promised.

"Get serious," she said.

Adam wasn't sure if she was talking to him or to the man back in New York. He'd been flippant, but now that he thought about it, the idea of Kris Jackson perched across his thighs was an event he looked forward to instigating.

Halsey was being insistent himself.

"You're kidding," Kris said. "What difference does it make? He could look like Godzilla and you'd still want me wangling a deal, wouldn't you?"

If Halsey was defending himself, Adam couldn't hear the man's oration. But the expression on Kris's face grew more and more content.

"Maybe I'll just have to go off on my own," she said, her voice theatrically reluctant. She listened a moment or so longer, her smile growing more and more like that of the Cheshire cat in *Alice in Wonderland*.

"Well," Kris admitted as if loath to give in on any point. "You could give me the number of that talent agency in LA. The one that represents rock bands."

She helped herself to the pen in Adam's desk set and scribbled a name and a couple of California phone numbers on a convenient pad. "From the Pen of Roidan Ryder" the scrap proclaimed in Klakith crude graphics.

Halsey was excited again. "All right," Kris said. "I'll give you a chance to redeem yourself, Halsey. I won't call Sanderson. Yet. No, Ryder isn't convinced life on the road would agree with him." She gave Adam a level glance. "Not yet at any rate. I'll keep in touch."

Kris returned the receiver to the cradle and folded the paper with her newly acquired phone numbers in half.

"You play baseball?" she asked.

"I like tennis better," Adam said.

"I'll give you a choice, then. I've got two men on base at this point. Or it's forty love."

"That confident?"

"Damn right, Cheney. Dean Taggart is as good as on a whistle-stop trip of his own. If his band is only half decent I'll pull in enough favors to get them on the road doing one-nighters in two-horse towns. He's a good-looking kid. Which means there will be eager little trollops hanging on his every word."

She was either very good at her job or one hell of a con artist. Adam almost believed that Taggart would fall victim to the lure of semi-success.

Almost.

Kris didn't know the young man as well as he did. Or the Taggart family. Despite the blatant come-on tactics of Roxie Taggart, Dean's young aunt, the Taggarts were all salt-of-the-earth souls. Taggart's father had never had high ambitions. As long as his family was provided for, the man was content. Dean was cut from the same cloth as his old man. No one had ever asked him to spend his free time at Klakith Lodge doing the daily jobs that Adam himself had usually handled during the off-season.

Adam wondered what he would have done without Dean Taggart and his cheerful assumption of chores the last four months. He'd taken care of the horses, not only exercising the big bay gelding, but doing heavier jobs like forking hay from the loft or cleaning the stalls. He'd even been on hand to carry in a ton of groceries when Lyanne had gotten hold of her first batch of manufacturers' coupons and gone on a spending spree at the market.

There were so many things a man on crutches couldn't do. Simple things. And Dean Taggart had swooped down like a hawk, taking advantage of Adam's temporary affliction.

Which was an ungrateful reaction to another man's good heart, Adam thought. Well, he was petty and couldn't help wanting revenge on Dean for taking center stage in Lyanne's life. A spot Adam himself had held for ten years. He was jealous of the attention she gave Dean Taggart. Fearful that Lyanne would no longer need him, that she would grow up and leave him with an emptiness in his life.

She was more than just a sister to him. She was his daughter. It wasn't easy to see another man reflected in her eyes—in her heart.

It wasn't very chivalrous to nurture the vicious flaw in his personality. He'd written Klakith as a reflection of his own philosophies. Or so he'd thought. His own characters would never show such unwarranted pettiness, though. They had higher ideals, better morals than he possessed. He should try to be more like Dalwulf and his ilk.

Instead, the idea that Kris Jackson would soon succeed in tearing Lyanne and Taggart apart cheered him immensely.

He watched her, still perched on the corner of his desk, one foot swinging idly. "That sure of yourself?" Adam asked.

"Absolutely." She nearly smirked with satisfaction. "Want me to drag your luggage out of storage?"

"It's not over yet, slick," he reminded. "I wouldn't start celebrating yet."

"So cautious," Kris admonished. "You ever do anything without thinking about it for days, Cheney?"

"I'm not a spontaneous person. I'm methodical."

Kris got off the desk and dropped down on the chair by the window. She made herself at home, pulling the lever that stretched the upright into a lounger. "Did it ever occur to you that some people might find that a bit stifling? Perhaps even boring?"

"Like you?" he suggested. The desk chair tilted back into a recliner as well. Adam pulled the footrest into position and leaned back, his cast now supported in comfort rather than dragging on the floor. "There's a lot of pleasure to be gained in thinking about a thing leisurely before actually acting."

"Is there really?"

Like kissing you, Adam answered silently. He had thought of little else since he'd first seen her towering indignantly over him down at the dock. Yes, the vision of not only kissing Kris Jackson, but of having her respond to each caress had kept him awake most of the night. He hadn't let the dream stagnate there, though. He'd moved it on to a time when he could chart every inch of her at his leisure.

The only problem he had foreseen in the whole scenario was how to make the fantasy come true. There were too many stumbling-blocks. Lyanne's presence, his cast, the lack of opportunity. And, of course, there was Kris's cooperation in the scheme as well. After the way she'd behaved earlier, though, Adam had great hopes that her involvement would be as enthusiastic as his own.

"I can be as spontaneous as the next guy," Adam insisted, "when it comes to buying a candy bar at the checkout stand. But where my life-style is involved, I'll take careful plotting every time."

"Thus speaks the writer," Kris announced. She crossed her ankles and stretched her arms above her head. "How much planning do you think went into my little con job on Halsey a moment ago?"

Adam laughed. "Years of experience, probably. How long have you known him?"

"Too long," she said, and stifled a yawn. Outside the window she had a clear view of the lake and the forestland beyond it. The sky was a dull, even gray. The whole setting was depressing and cold. "Looks like it's going to snow," Kris offered.

"Naw. Those are rain clouds. Didn't you know it's spring, slick?"

Kris sighed. "Ah, yes. So it is. Horrible time of year. I want sunshine and tropical temperatures." She folded her arms across her chest and snuggled back into the deep upholstery of the chair. "I want to be warm again."

Adam's chair squeaked as he adjusted the setting, causing the footrest to rise another inch. "That's not the sentiment of a Normass warrior." At her silence, he explained. "All Normass women are warriors, you know."

"Yeah. I know. Good old stalwart Emling. The perfect woman, huh? I'll bet she can fry an egg, burp a baby, and hold off a horde of Klakithian wildebeests all in a single movement." Kris covered another yawn. "You and your damn fantasy women got us in this spot, Cheney. Can't you control your baser self?"

"Instincts are hard to squelch, slick. Sort of like the rapier edge of your wayward tongue."

"My answer to Emling's broadsword, no doubt," she murmured. Kris closed her eyes. The warmth of the lodge was wonderfully restful. She could almost feel the tension easing from her tight muscles. Unconscious of her actions, Kris wiggled deeper into the cushions. "Still, why couldn't you have used a plump little broad-beamed kelly green Resedian for your dream girl?"

Adam lay back in his own chair, amused to find his guest was showing a reluctant preference for his company. Her call had been completed and still she lingered with no apparent intention of returning to her own cabin. In fact, from the lazy tone of her voice, it sounded distinctly like Kris was about to fall asleep in his armchair.

"Emling isn't my dream girl," Adam said. "I created her for Dalwulf."

"Don't . . . quibble," Kris murmured, drowsily. "Your sister assures . . . says . . . you are . . . Wulfy." The last word was barely audible.

Adam waited a minute or so, watching the way Kris lay, her head tucked into the wing of the chair, her face turned from the soft light of the window.

"Slick?" he asked.

Only the faint rise and fall of her breast answered.

Quietly, Adam switched off the long-ignored computer and eased from his own chair. There was a folded stadium rug on one of the lower bookshelves. A reminder of the high-school sporting events he'd dutifully attended with Lyanne in the past. She hadn't even asked him to go last fall. Instead, her friends had come up the mountain to pick her up.

Adam balanced carefully, moving without the aid of his crutches, something he could only manage in the close confines of the office where there were numerous pieces of furniture to lean against. He opened the rug, dropping it lightly over Kris's sleeping form.

thirteen

THE SKY WAS A THREATENING ORANGE GLOW, ITS TONE nearly a match for the tall spires of rock that thrust like needles toward the burning heavens. She pressed closer to the stone, knowing that her coloring made her an all-too-easily-seen target. Where were the cool blues and icy whites of her world? The drifts of downy-soft snow or the chill dampness of an enchanted cavern with its ageless stalactites and stalagmites? The only white in this world was the paleness of her own short hair, of the chalk dust that covered the man's leg, disguising his injury. Of the fear in her wide, rounded eyes.

He was too near. They were too near. Too insistent that she travel with this alien man. A man with warm skin the color of lightly browned bread. A man with the eyes of a wolf, and hair the hue of the sunrise in this hated world of hot pigments and even hotter tempers.

Kris squinted her eyes against the glare of the red sun

that baked the cursed Middle World. She stirred in her sleep, sheltering in the imaginary lee of a sandstone pinnacle, hiding from the insistent men of Asteroid Books and Starburst Pictures who wanted her to lure Roidan Ryder from the shelter of these hills and into the world.

Not Ryder. Adam. The man in her dream held a stance similar to those chosen for Dalwulf the Dealer on the covers of the Klakith books. And still high above, the merciless red sun beat down.

Red. As red as blood, as rich as the rusty-brown color of Adam's hair. Thick, soft, and . . . And she was a Normass woman, wasn't she? She should not feel this strange longing to be held by this barbarian from another land. But she did. And when he stepped back into the shelter of the soaring sandstone, she went readily into his arms, burying her cheek against that intoxicatingly alien mane. And when he kissed her . . . licked her . . .

Kris sat up abruptly. The Irish setter leaped onto her lap and lovingly washed Kris's face again.

Finding her fingers buried in the deep red fur of the dog's winter coat, Kris hastily pushed the eager pet away and levered the chair upright. A stadium blanket slid to the floor. Kris bent to retrieve it, folding it across the back of the chair.

"You didn't cover me up, did you?" she asked the setter.

The dog panted eagerly and pushed her nose into Kris's hand, nudging her to continue her earlier, unconscious caresses.

Kris gave in to the look in the pooch's big brown eyes. "This is not good," Kris mumbled. "I mean, you may think so at the moment. Try not to drool on my slacks, would you? But look at it from my perspective. If some AKC stud gave you the look . . . you know what I mean, right?"

The setter murmured something in answer.

"Absolutely," Kris agreed. "*That* look. Makes you feel the tides, and hear things growing. Makes your backbone about as stiff as a piece of overcooked pasta. Makes you short of breath all the time."

Again the dog indicated that she was in complete accord with her newfound friend.

Kris rubbed the setter's thick coat, scratching just behind the long flopping ears. "So what would you do?" she asked.

The dog considered a moment, then hunched her rump closer to Kris.

"Is that merely because it's spring? I mean, there is something about this time of year . . . even here in the mountains . . . that makes one's mind naturally turn toward . . ."

This time the dog indicated her opinion with a more audible reply.

"You have to be a little more articulate than just woof," Kris pointed out.

A giggle filled the room just before Lyanne bounced in through the open doorway. "She said if you're hungry I can fix you some lunch," the girl explained. She dropped down on the floor and the dog bounded off the lounger, ready for more active exercise than discussing men with Kris.

"You must have been really tired," Lyanne said. "Adam said you dropped off in the middle of a sentence so we let you sleep through lunch. It turned out to be such a nice day, Adam decided to fish instead of work." She wrestled the Irish setter to the floor, rolling the dog over on her back to expose the softer coat of her belly. Lyanne scratched, finding a spot that had Kris's confidante's hind leg twitching.

Kris glanced out the window, out at the stretch of lake and sky and trees. The clouds had broken and the sun had come out. It had been the warm rays on her face that had set her dream in motion, turning her into Emling. It had to be!

Kris swung her legs to the floor and stood up. "I'll be fine. I usually don't have lunch."

Lyanne nodded, still playing with the dog. "Good girl," she approved, still scratching. "Were you a good shrink?"

"Which of us are you talking to?" Kris asked, her voice slightly amused. "Me or the dog? What's her name, anyway? I've never heard anyone call her."

"Oh, we don't. She's got her own schedule, don't you, sweetheart?"

The setter's tongue lolled in pleasure.

Lyanne giggled. "Her name's Honey," she said. "I named her but Adam said . . ." Her voice dropped in a poor imitation of her brother's deep tones. "If you think I'm going to yell *Honey* out the door and have some dog answer, you've got another think coming." She giggled again. "He did once and I fell on the floor laughing, he sounded so funny."

The dog decided to wash her young mistress's face.

"Yes, I know you love me," Lyanne cooed.

Kris dropped down on the floor next to the ecstatic pair. "What did you mean about being a good shrink?"

"Oh, that? It's because you were talking to Honey just like Adam does. He says she's highly skilled at sorting out the problems of others."

Kris took the dog's muzzle in her hand and met the soft look in the setter's eyes. "You didn't tell me that, did you?" she accused the shaggy canine.

Honey mumbled something under her breath and tried to lick Kris's hand in appeasement.

Lyanne trilled happily. "I think she just claimed confidentiality between patient and doctor."

Those big brown dog eyes appeared to have a touch of

unholy humor in them as far as Kris was concerned. "Just to be on the safe side," she said, "I think I'll keep my dreams to myself from now on."

She was still bothered by the dream and the nagging feeling that she'd been gypped of something very special when the setter's affectionate greeting had awoken her. Of course, that was ridiculous. The only reason she'd dreamed that she was Emling of Normass, in danger and protected by Dalwulf the Dealer (complete with white cast), was that she'd been reading too many of the Klakith novels.

So what had she done when she'd had enough of Lyanne and the dog? She'd returned to her own cabin and opened yet another book.

It was impossible not to hear and see Adam Cheney in every word or action of his protagonist. And after that stupid dream, reading of Dalwulf's involvement with various beauties made Kris distinctly jealous.

Lord! What had the man done to her? She was a total wreck. And worse! She'd been the one to instigate that embrace on the stairs earlier. She was the one dreaming of being a Klakithian heroine eager to fall in his arms at the slightest provocation.

Halsey. It was all Halsey's fault. If he hadn't sent her on this ridiculous assignment . . .

No, it was Belinda's fault. If her mother wasn't always so insistent on matchmaking, then . . .

Kris curled up against the headboard of the bed in her cabin. The Franklin stove was working beautifully now that she'd been given the secret to its success. She returned all the bedding, creating a far more comfortable nest on the mattress. Surrounded by pillows and blankets, Kris felt nicely barricaded against the elements. And somehow decadent. All she could think about were the piles of softly cured pelts that served as bedding in Normass and what it would be like to play-act, pretending to be Emling in fact, rather than just in coloring . . .

. . . which treacherous thought led her back in a dangerous circle to the surely unnatural attraction she felt for Adam Cheney.

Wouldn't Belinda be obnoxiously bright about her daughter's affliction? *Damn right, she would be*, Kris thought viciously. Oh, she'd fancied herself in love in the past, but she'd never been this drawn to any man before. She wasn't sure she wanted to be. While other women panted for a chance to attract Tasker Fane's attention, she'd been panting in the effort to escape such familiarity. Fane was an A-number-one creep and women seemed to eat up his casual use and roving eye.

A man didn't have to be a star to take what he wanted and run. Hadn't numerous stepfathers played the same part, merely against a different backdrop? There'd even been the one who decided he had struck the jackpot, gaining two beautiful stepdaughters under his roof in addition to a lovely wife. Kris had been Lyanne's age that year and too afraid to tell her mother about the man's eager hands. Her sister Sandy had no such compunction. She'd crowned the creep and packed both herself and Kris off to a friend's house.

Kris rolled over on her stomach and hugged one of the pillows tightly. What she wouldn't have given to have Sandy there next to her. Sandy had always known what she wanted and had gone after it. She'd set her sights on Charles Ballard and planned the campaign to catch him. Within six months of meeting, the two had been wed. Sandy had never looked back. Kris doubted her sister had any regrets.

"How did you know he was the one?" she'd pestered

Sandy once. "I mean, *really* the one? Mom always thinks she's found the perfect man, and they never are."

Sandy had laughed, her voice as light and frivolous-sounding as Belinda's. It was the only thing that Sandy had inherited from their mother. "That's because she hasn't learned that there is no such thing as a perfect man. She keeps hoping but, of course, she's always disappointed."

"So Charles is flawed?" Kris had asked of her brother-in-law.

"Wonderfully flawed," his wife had agreed. "But so am I, Krissy. Just in different ways. Together we function like a well-oiled cog, our flawed gears meeting and working in harmony."

Sandy claimed it was one of the many wonderful things she'd learned from her stepmother, her real father's second, and far more enduring wife. As much as Kris loved Belinda, she occasionally envied Sandy's relationship with another woman.

Kris punched the pillow and wondered if the Irish setter was busy. She could use a friendly ear, even if it was a long shaggy one.

Flawed. Well, that word certainly fit Adam Cheney's personality. The man was ridiculously overprotective when it came to his little sister. He retreated from the world, not just to this mountain wilderness, but into a land of his own creation. A strange planet with a red sun.

Hell. Didn't Cheney know anything? Look at comic book history! Hadn't Krypton exploded when its red sun had gone nova? Superman's parents had sent him hurtling into space to save him. Dalwulf wouldn't use science to do so. He'd probably be dumb enough to just hurl his son Earthward hoping the toss reached the Kent homestead.

No, he wouldn't. That was unkind. And if there was one thing Kris knew about Adam, it was that the man was terribly intelligent. She read it in his stories. Reluctantly. It would have been so much better to see him as a cad, as just another Tasker Fane to be flattered and avoided. But she couldn't do that.

What she should have done was leave, not accept that ridiculous challenge to tame Lyanne. Why had she picked up that particular gauntlet? She'd turned her back on taunts before, on deals that shady celebrities had proposed.

Kris rolled over on her back, still clutching the pillow. She knew exactly why she'd accepted Adam's deal. It was because he'd touched her. And ever since she'd been suffering from the worst case of moonsickness ever known in the chronicles of Klakith.

The intoxicating smell of fresh bread wafted throughout the lodge when Kris returned later that evening. There was no one in the front room or the office, so Kris followed her nose out to the kitchen. There the scent of broiling chicken entwined with the perfume of baking bread. Adam was lounging at the table, his cast propped on one of the side chairs. The dog was curled up nearby, sound asleep, immune to the sounds of brother and sister bickering.

The subject under discussion dealt with the relative merits of canned asparagus over frozen broccoli. Neither sounded particularly appealing to Kris. When asked her opinion she suggested green beans. By mutual agreement everyone did without a vegetable.

It was a pleasant meal. No one mentioned Klakith, movie tours, or what was really on their minds. Occasionally Lyanne looked dreamy, which Kris put down to the girl's penchant for Dean Taggart and an afternoon spent with him in the barn. Adam looked thoughtful, as if he were brooding on something. His golden wolf eyes occasionally alighted on her, but Kris couldn't read his expression. For her own part, Kris concentrated on polishing off her dinner and a good share of the heavenly bread. She felt absolutely decadent as melted butter dripped from her final slice.

Adam watched her, his eyes following her actions when she licked butter from the corner of her mouth, then from her fingers. Kris couldn't imagine doing either at her own house (but then she never cooked), or at her mother's (where everything was so formal). But at Klakith Lodge life was far more relaxed. She'd never been part of such a cozy setting before. While both the Cheneys rushed at some aspects of life, they knew how to enjoy quiet moments and casual companionship. Watching them tease each other, Kris found it hard to believe that Lyanne was so anxious to grow up or that Adam was adamantly opposed to her doing so. Despite their laid-back living arrangements, neither was willing to let time cure their problems.

And then there was Kris Jackson, devil's advocate, to plague this narrow paradise.

The Cheneys were at peace with each other, seemingly content to let events swirl around them unnoticed that evening. Their easy affection made Kris feel like an outsider, nose pressed to the window, a street urchin longing to be part of their circle of affection.

The dishes had been cleared, but they still all lingered at the table. The coffeepot was nearly empty when Lyanne announced that they had planned a special entertainment for Kris that night.

"We're going to make Adam's special taffy," Lyanne announced enthusiastically.

Adam gave Kris a sheepish smile. "My taffy is much acclaimed at slumber parties in this stretch of the woods."

"It is!" Lyanne agreed. "When Marissa had her sleepover she was really upset when her mother wouldn't invite Adam, too, just so we could have a taffy pull."

Kris blinked. "A taffy pull?"

Adam grinned over at his sister. "City slicker, Lye. She'll probably balk at touching it."

"Touch it? You aren't kidding! How sanitary is this?"

"Only one rule, slick. If you drop it on the floor, it belongs to the dog."

Kris frowned, still not sure whether they were just teasing.

"You do like taffy, don't you?" Lyanne asked.

"Sure." All wrapped up in paper from Atlantic City.

Adam issued orders in a quick succession that had his sister gathering ingredients and placing them near the stove top. Putting his crutches aside, Adam balanced on his good leg and tossed together his specialty in a large pot. When the concoction was boiling like the contents of a witch's cauldron, Lyanne objected.

"You forgot the secret words."

His brows rose in theatrical contempt. "Whose brew is this? I chanted them silently in deference to Ms. Jackson."

Lyanne giggled. "Afraid it will scare her off?"

"She hasn't displayed enough imagination to make it convincing," he said. "Plus, we're lacking a gift."

Kris wasn't to be put off. "What gift?"

The steam rising from the candy mixture gave Adam the hazy appearance of a wizard. He was into his character now. He waved his hands over the pseudo-cauldron and chanted a series of nonsensical words. They all began with harsh "K" sounds.

"The gift, the precious gift, handed down from the shamans of old, of this world and that . . ." Adam continued.

Lyanne joined in. Kris watched in amazement as the girl curled her legs in a Lotus position, rested her wrists limply on her outstretched knees and closed her eyes.

"The gift, the precious gift," the teenager chanted, her

voice serious where Adam's was accented with a hint of humor.

"The favored will be given, the favored will receive, the favored will rejoice," Adam intoned, and winked at Kris. "If you aren't in the sacred position you won't be among the favored, slick."

Kris assumed the Lotus and waited to see what happened next in this strange ceremony from the planet Klakith. She had no doubt that somewhere in her reading of the chronicles she would come upon a similar ceremony.

"Is it allowed to ask what gift the favored will be given?" she asked.

Lyanne didn't open her eyes or move, but it was she who answered while her brother performed another magical swipe or so with his hands over his concoction. "Depends," the girl said. "At the slumber parties it was usually a reading of a past life. Adam always made them adventurous, romantic, and silly. But when Becky and I did it at Marissa's sixteenth birthday party the gifts were kisses. From boys," she added unnecessarily.

"Obviously," Adam said, "I wasn't invited to that party either."

Lyanne giggled but kept her stance, eyes closed, arms extended, palms up as if she chanted a mantra. Then she resumed the monotonous tone to make a request. "And what is the gift for your favored this holy eve, weaver of epics?"

"Not kisses, I hope," Kris murmured.

"Spoilsport." Adam dipped a wooden spoon in his mixture and held it high before tipping the ingredients back into the pot. "I suppose you aren't interested in your past life either."

"Depends on whether I was Cleopatra or Napoleon's Josephine," Kris said.

Adam stirred his cauldron. "I was thinking more along the lines of a sniveling guttersnipe who rises to fame on the smock tails of a famous painter when he immortalizes her beauty."

Lyanne sighed.

Adam watched Kris, one brow raised speculatively. "Naw. That won't work," he decided at last. He allowed the cooking candy a moment of further consideration. "No, in honor of Ms. Jackson's stay we should have a special treat. What say you, neophyte sister of the brew?"

"Whatever your wish is," Lyanne intoned after a moment's thought.

"Think, little acolyte," he urged. "My wish doesn't count. Our guest already nixed that."

Lyanne thought a moment. "Well, kisses wouldn't be any fun since Dean isn't here," she agreed.

"Speak for yourself, minx," Adam said. "If you don't think of something soon, the magic sweets will be ready to handle."

"Okay." Lyanne's brow creased, her eyes squeezed closed tighter. "There is one gift that has not been given in a long time," she said. "The gift of the imaginary magic-carpet journey, like Mommy used to invent."

Adam growled one of his harsh-sounding Klakith words. When Lyanne's eyes flew open, he shrugged and claimed to have burnt his finger. Kris had been watching him, though, and knew that Adam's movements had been too precise and careful for him to have accidentally burnt himself. For a moment there she'd thought he'd been in pain. Mental pain.

"Too late," he announced. "Taffy's ready for cooling." Lyanne hopped up immediately to hand him a series of buttered, shallow bowls.

fourteen

KRIS WATCHED, WAITING FOR A HINT OF THE SHADOW she'd read in Adam's eyes to reappear. But it didn't. It continued to be a lighthearted session with Lyanne determined to play, and Adam playfully avoiding being serious.

Although she'd never pulled taffy before, Kris soon found her hands had been coated with melted butter and she had a glob of clear, cooling candy in her palm. Lyanne was eager in her demonstration of how to pull the substance until it was a creamy ivory in tone. Then she cut her finished article into bite-sized pieces and rushed on to another batch before it got too cool to work easily.

Kris tugged her candy back and forth, first from one hand to another, then back again. Slowly it began to transform.

"Not fast enough, slick," Adam admonished. His large hands handled the goop easily, working further magic as his candy took on the hue of . . . of . . . a Normass ice castle,

Kris thought. Hell, she was really stuck in this Klakith mind frame.

In fury, she yanked at the candy harder, only to have it break and straggle down her arm, making her skin sticky. In almost the same instant, the phone rang and Lyanne was off like a shot for the office, leaving Kris and Adam alone.

Kris scraped a reluctant string of taffy from her arm and worked it back into the batch in her hand. She was still on her first bowl of candy where Lyanne and Adam had both gone on to their third by now.

"You really hate me, don't you?" she said.

"Because I forced you to pull taffy?" Adam grinned over at her. After the cooking pot had been emptied and set aside in the sink to soak, he had returned to his chair. It had edged a bit closer to hers as the evening progressed.

Taffy trailing from her fingers, Kris nodded. "Look at me. I'm a mess."

"You're beautiful," he said.

"Tell me something original, Cheney. How am I supposed to get this stuff off?" She held up one hand. "I look webbed."

He studied her fingers. Long, slender, ringless fingers. Attached to narrow wrists, their tracing of veins was covered with skin so pale and translucent it rivaled the graceful alabaster statues of the ancients.

"You didn't use enough butter on your hands. Now there's only one way to free yourself," Adam said. He set his finished length of taffy aside on a sheet of waxed paper and took her hand. His eyes never leaving hers, Adam licked Kris's palm.

And something in Kris snapped. She was sure that he could feel her shaking, could hear the hoarseness of her breath as it rattled in her throat.

It was an effort to speak. She forced the words out, was surprised when they sounded normal.

"You're living dangerously," Kris murmured.

"Eating sweets?"

"No. In using innuendos around your sister. She's going to think you want to kiss me."

"Want to? Going to," he warned.

There was actual fluttering going on beneath her rib cage now, as if the wild cardinals had strayed there and been trapped. Something untamed certainly hammered within.

"I thought that you didn't want to give your sister ideas," Kris tried.

"I don't."

His smile could be so utterly charming at times. And so devastatingly wicked at others. It was definitely the latter now. Against her wishes, Kris's gaze dropped to the devilish curve and the glint of bright white teeth.

"Then we shouldn't . . ." she began.

"Dawdle," Adam finished. "She could be back any moment."

His fingers were still slick with butter and a hint of candy. They left a sweet trail both in sugar and sensation as they played along Kris's chin and jawline.

Kris tried again. "But . . ."

Adam had been lying in wait. As soon as her lips parted, his mouth claimed hers, his tongue sliding easily between the soft welcoming gates. Kris leaned toward him. He tasted of the candy he'd licked from her hand. The wizard's magical taffy. Surely it was the spell he cast over the cauldron that made her feel so lightheaded, so reckless.

When they parted, Kris took a long, ragged breath. "Of course, a kiss is all there can ever be," she said. "Because of Lyanne."

Adam didn't lean back in his chair immediately but continued to fondle her cheek. His touch lingered with a sticky reluctance. "She heard about this afternoon," he said. "Dean described our cozy little scene. Lye told me quite seriously that she approves."

"Of me knocking you down?"

He revised the scenario. "Of you throwing yourself at me."

Kris jerked away from him. "Throwing myself at you! You . . . you . . ."

Adam leaned back, quite content with his world. "She did think you were being a bit drastic in your efforts to get me on the road to promote the movie."

"What!" Kris couldn't sit still any longer. She surged to her feet, started to run her hands through her short hair and stopped just shy, remembering their candy-coated condition. She could still taste the faint flavor of taffy on her lips from his kiss. Still feel the warm intimacy of Adam's tongue against her palm. Kris strode over to the sink and washed both the candy and the caress away.

"You let her think that I would . . . would consort with clients just to . . ."

"Don't forget her favorite photo," Adam chided. "You were pretty cozy with that Fane guy."

Kris finished with her hands, found a dishcloth, and scrubbed at the sticky tracks on her face, washing the lingering warmth of Adam's touch away. "He was limping a few seconds later," she growled.

"Hmm. I must remember that."

"Do," Kris stormed and headed for the door.

Adam's voice stopped her. "Kristine?"

Lord, she loved the way he said her name. It throbbed with an intent mystery. Like his earlier candy incantation, it was haunting. And promising.

She looked back, one hand against the swinging door. "Less than two days till I lose the cast," Adam said. "I won't let you run away quite so easily then."

Kris pushed out of the room, grabbed her fur, and headed for her now-cozy cabin. She hoped Adam didn't realize that she'd already started running more slowly.

She actually used the bed that night. Not that she slept at all. That was clearly impossible. Not because she was cold now, but because there was a nagging burning in the pit of her stomach. So Kris didn't sleep. She tossed and turned and wondered if Adam Cheney was as restless as she was.

It was barely dawn when Kris dared to try the shower. She found the water delightfully hot and the room far too cool when she left the narrow steamy stall. The fire in the Franklin stove had burned low. She shoved more wood into its hungry mouth and dressed quickly before its radiating warmth.

The main lodge would be much warmer. Kris wondered briefly how early the Cheneys rose on Sundays, but when she opened her cabin door she could hear music blaring from the open kitchen window. She was a little surprised to recognize Michael Bolton's hoarse voice. She'd grown so used to the heavy metal sounds Lyanne preferred.

Bolton's tones were much more to Kris's liking.

Once she was out the door, though, she was reluctant to head immediately for the lodge. Besides the music, the tempting smell of baking cinnamon rolls wafted her way. But, for just a moment, Kris wanted to savor the morning alone.

It was overcast. Clouds hung low, creating a veil of mist that concealed parts of the lake. Ghostly trails etched across the land. It was eerie, hushed, and beautiful. The water lapped peacefully at the shore. The air was fresh, clear, and broken only by the sound of birds in the nearby trees. As Kris drew nearer to the lake, she noticed the little cardinal couple had come down close to the shoreline to look for their breakfast.

To avoid disturbing them, Kris altered her course, passing through and into the swirling mist down near the pier. She leaned on one of the pilings, unaware of the odd picture she made, a woman in an expensive fur coat framed by the rustic, weathered wharf, and the gray elements of mist, lake, and sky.

Whatever she did today, there was no turning back. She could go with Lyanne to listen to Dean's band rehearse, then call the numbers Halsey had given her in Los Angeles. That would get Dean away from the girl and all that remained was to guide Lyanne in a more appropriate choice of clothing. Once she'd accomplished the "taming" of Cheney's sister, he would be honor-bound to go on the publicity tour. Her job would be done.

Or she could end the job now. Just go back to the cabin, pack everything back in the BMW and drive away from Klakith Lodge. Her conscience would be clear then. She'd pushed a number of people around while on tours, always for their own good, but sticking her nose in Lyanne Cheney's life wasn't quite the same thing. Oh, guiding the girl's taste in clothing wouldn't be either difficult or traumatic. But how did Kris know that separating the girl from Dean Taggart wouldn't be devastating? First love was very fragile. By tampering with it, who knew down what road she would be urging Lyanne? Kris didn't want the girl's future on her conscience.

If Adam hadn't suggested the ridiculous proposition she wouldn't be in this spot. And now that he'd kissed her, Kris wondered if she had accepted merely because fulfilling their stupid bargain gave her an excuse to stay near him.

She'd liked that kiss far too much. It had been . . . what? Not earth-shattering. Kris didn't believe passions could be that strong. But it had certainly been . . . been . . . nice.

What a pastel kind of word for something so . . . so . . . Damn it! Nice!

Of course, if she stayed, there was not only the chance that she'd ruin Lyanne's life, there was the chance that Adam would kiss her again. When balanced on scales that way, it should be easy to choose the right course. Except Adam's spell threw the scales out of kilter.

Kris pulled her coat collar up around her throat and turned to work her way back to the lodge. It was illogical, probably immoral as well, yet there had never been any real doubt as to which course she would take. The scales didn't balance right. One side had been weighted by a taffy-flavored magic kiss.

Lord, she was already addicted to his kisses. She really should leave, stop tempting fate. Just throw in the towel, go back to New York and book a deck chair on the next Windjammer. Then she could forget Adam Cheney, his sister, and Klakith. She would save herself a lot of trouble. She could prevent what she feared would happen. She'd guarded against the possibility for so long, keeping a wall between herself and the men she dated. It couldn't happen to her now, not at Klakith Lodge.

She didn't want to fall in love.

When he couldn't sleep, Adam usually made good use of his insomnia by working. But even extricating Dalwulf and Emling from a tight spot hadn't been enough to keep his mind off Kris Jackson.

For a man who had no future of his own planned, it was a dangerous thing to keep dwelling on the loveliness of one particular woman. It made him fantasize about what a normal life would have been like, one where he wasn't bound by responsibilities.

If he had not become Lyanne's guardian all those years ago, would he have created the aura of mystery around Roidan Ryder? Would he even have created an alter ego to front for his work? He was proud of the Klakith tales. Proud of the world he'd created and the creatures who inhabited it. There was depth to his characters, a warm, caring side that not all readers recognized. They were the ones who saw Dalwulf's activities in the bride trade as something akin to slavery. He saw merely a man who was paid to protect women en route to the men who would care for them. If Dalwulf fell a little in love with each of the women in his care, it merely meant he was human. But in the end he had nothing to offer them. No security, no life, no abiding affection. Dalwulf hadn't found anything in the succession of lovely heroines that would bind him to one of them for life.

Not until Emling, that is.

Nor had he, Adam mused, until Kristine Jackson.

He was no different from the hero he had created. If Dalwulf had nothing to offer Emling, what had Adam to offer Kris? She was a woman used to the fast life of the city. A woman who ran even faster in her chosen profession. Could she slow down to the quiet sameness of each day at Klakith Lodge? He feared she'd laugh if he ever suggested it.

Or would that be like caging a wild bird? She would wilt and slowly lose that vibrancy that attracted him so. Yet, until Lyanne graduated and moved on to college, he was trapped in a cage himself, bound to the home he'd made for his sister at Klakith Lodge.

It wasn't that he wasn't happy there. But there were times when the bright lights still drew him. As they had when he was young. He no longer felt young. The fourteen years that separated him from his sister had forced him to age beyond his years. He was barely thirty. Yet he felt forty, fifty. A hundred years old at times.

If only . . .

The phrase had allowed him to imagine himself out of numerous tight spots on Klakith, those innumerable times when the characters changed the scenario on him and let him write himself into a corner. Now "if only" was the phrase that started nearly all his thoughts.

If only the Klakith movie deal had happened two years down the road and he'd met Kris when he was free again.

If only he hadn't given in to temptation and kissed her.

If only she hadn't responded to his touch with that startled, then entranced surrender. It had been just a flash, a sudden dropping of the shields that protected her, before they were back in place, as strong as the walls of any Klakithian fortress.

But he'd been inside those ramparts and the woman within had proven to be a more powerful sorceress than he'd expected. She'd cast a spell, then cast him back into the world of mortal fools.

He would storm the gate, break through the portcullis and find the woman who did more than warm his blood. He would claim the woman who enchanted his mind.

He could lay riches at her feet, but even the treasures of a monarchy would not interest her. Kris had a successful career of her own. She didn't need him to have security.

She was a gorgeous woman, tall, stately, sure of herself and of her reception in the world. She'd been petted and pampered. He was sure of it. Her brand of sophistication was developed in elite salons, not in back-road places like his hometown.

They were complete opposites. She'd lived a life of luxury. She thought nothing of splurging on furs, frequent holidays. He knew what it meant to grovel for everything he got, still found himself counting pennies even though his bank account was more than healthy now. Old habits died hard. He still put Lyanne's welfare before his own. Kris appeared to be unencumbered by family.

There were some things he and Kris had in common, though. They'd started at different levels, but they'd both made a mark for themselves in their professions. If her credentials hadn't checked out, the producers and publishers wouldn't have hired her. The fact that she had a surface resemblance to Emling had merely been a plus. He was sure that they would have sent her, no matter what she looked like. She had a reputation for doing the impossible. And he'd long been considered impossible when it came to personal appearances.

In the kitchen Lyanne was giving her all to Michael Bolton's rendition of "Georgia On My Mind." Adam could smell breakfast, the cinnamon rolls a special addition to the usual Sunday fare in honor of their guest. But he wasn't ready to share the morning with his perky little sister. Not yet. Instead, crutches in hand, he maneuvered quietly to the front door and went out on the porch.

The swirling morning mist made his private kingdom look like Arthur's Avalon, or the enchanted heights of the Normass mountains. Mysterious, promising, yet gloomy.

Adam wished things could be as simple as they were on Klakith. In a land where oracles still practiced their trade, he would have asked for a sign. Something to tell him if his instincts were right. Or if he'd just been sleeping alone for too long.

On Klakith, destiny was written in the dawn. The sun had yet to fight clear of the clouds. Yet soon the cloaking mists would be gone. With them would go the chance of a sign. It was thus on Klakith. It would be the same for him.

Adam stared out toward the lake, at the swirling fingers of mist. And just as it had occurred for Dalwulf the Dealer numerous pages ago in *The Warrior Bride* manuscript, Adam was given a sign. He saw his own destiny.

Coming toward him slowly through the mist was the tall, stately, fur-clad form of Kristine Jackson.

fifteen

ALTHOUGH DAWN WAS PASSING ON EARTH, IN ADAM'S mind all the promise of Kakert, the night on which the two moons of Klakith mated, had been fulfilled. He knew what he wanted, knew that he could have it all with just a little planning. All it took was a clever plot, superb execution, and time.

The creation of the character Emling hadn't been merely a ploy to end the Klakith chronicles. It had been to assuage a need in himself. So he'd pictured the type of woman he preferred. Not someone with the sweet domestic ways of his late mother, not a curvaceous airhead such as his sister had become, but a cool woman of the world, a warrior in her own right, A Normass woman with a heart as stalwart as her consort's, and a hidden passion that only one man could unleash.

He'd been dreaming. Emling had been the result. He'd never expected her to walk into his life.

But she had. The more he knew of Kris Jackson, the more she appeared to resemble the character he'd invented. But Kris was more than Emling would ever be, just as Dalwulf was only a small part of him, the better part. Adam hadn't the Dealer's high morals, though. He was determined to win the woman from New York even if he had to be underhanded in his methods.

Perhaps he needn't be, though. He remembered the sweet surprise of their briefly shared kiss. Time. That's what he needed. He hoped there would be sufficient. Kris Jackson seemed to work at a much swifter pace than he did.

Kris couldn't ever remember having spent a Sunday morning quite like this one before. So often she'd been up late the night before with tour duties or a party she'd felt obligated to attend. Sunday had been for sleeping late. When she visited her sister Sandra in Connecticut, the routine was early rising, hasty grooming of three children, and a family trip to church followed by brunch at a restaurant.

But at Klakith the pace was relaxed. The Cheneys lingered at their table, passing fresh cinnamon rolls and sections of the Sunday paper back and forth. They'd included her in their intimate little circle as if she weren't an outsider plotting to upset their quiet world.

It made her quandary all the worse. She hated the idea of deceiving Lyanne. She hated the idea of leaving Adam. If she backed out of the deal to tame his sister, though, there was no reason for her to stay. And to continue within the orbit of Adam's smile, she had to con his sister.

Lord, what a fool she was. After all these years, she was letting her attraction to a man rule her actions.

Of course, she could be blowing the whole thing out of proportion. The ploy to get Dean Taggart's band out of town semipermanently might backfire. Trite as it was, absence *had* been known to make the heart grow fonder. Taggart might have the guts to resist the band followers. If he didn't, who was to say that Lyanne would ever find he'd been unfaithful? They could be as devoted a couple when he returned as they were now. And no matter how much guidance Kris gave in pushing Lyanne toward a more sophisticated and conservative choice in dress, if Dean liked the slinky outfits, who was to say the girl wouldn't revert to them later?

But by that time Adam Cheney would already be out on tour pushing *Klakith*, the movie, and the book series. Her job would be a success, albeit a temporary one.

The more Kris thought about it, the more she was inclined to see this new line of thought as far more logical than her earlier sentimental reasoning. Human nature would revert to type no matter what kind of monkey wrench she threw in the way.

As a precaution, though, Kris made sure her chair at the table was far from Adam Cheney's.

Lyanne took the wheel for the drive into town later that afternoon. Adam bowed out of accompanying them, claiming his sister's driving strained his nerves. She laughed but didn't press him to change his mind.

"What's the city like?" the girl demanded of Kris not long after they'd left Klakith Lodge behind. "Adam and I lived in Los Angeles for awhile after Mommy and Daddy were . . . killed . . . but I don't remember much about it."

"You lived in LA?" Somehow she'd gotten the impression that the Cheneys had always lived on the mountain.

Lyanne nodded. Her long red-gold hair tossed a bit with the movement. "Adam moved there to go to college."

"Your brother went to UCLA?" How many more surprises were there to come?

"For awhile," the girl answered. "I can remember how California was all he talked about when I was little. How he couldn't wait to grow up and move away from Illinois."

Kris sat dully, stunned at the flow of information.

"Everyone was sick of hearing about UCLA and his plans. He was always going to be a writer, but it was for the movies and television back then."

"What happened?" Kris prompted when Lyanne paused.

"I don't remember much," the teen said. "I was only six when it happened. Adam says we'd all come out to visit him and there was an accident on the highway. I was asleep on the back seat and didn't get hurt. He'd been at school that day, and not with us. Mommy and Daddy were . . ." Her voice quavered. "Well, it was just Adam and me after that."

Kris touched the girl's shoulder. "I'm sorry I asked, Lyanne. I didn't mean to dredge up . . ."

"It's okay." The teenager had recovered already. "It was a long time ago. I don't miss them much. Why should I? Adam's always been there for me."

So it was an inflated sense of responsibility that made Cheney overprotective, Kris thought. She was playing at psychology in analyzing his actions, yet it was easy to understand Adam blaming himself for the loss. If he hadn't gone to California his parents wouldn't have come west to visit, and wouldn't have died on the Los Angeles freeway system.

It was time to change the subject, though. "I don't know a lot about LA," Kris admitted. "I've only visited. But New York is my home. I grew up there. What did you want to know about? Radio City Music Hall? The Staten Island Ferry? The plays on Broadway? The museums?"

Lyanne didn't hesitate. "The stores," she said. "I'd just like *die* if I could go shopping in New York."

After she finished laughing, Kris guided her young hostess verbally through Bloomingdale's, Saks Fifth Avenue, Macy's, and a few of the specialty stores. Judging that Ralph Lauren's western look would meet with Adam's approval, Kris painted an attractive picture of the designer's showroom for Lyanne.

The teenager's response was heartfelt. "Bitchin'," she said as they reached the outskirts of Cedar City. "What do you miss most when you're away?"

"Like now?" Kris thought a moment.

"Your friends?" Lyanne prompted.

Kris knew the answer wasn't that deep. There was something that she missed, something she'd fantasized about just that morning. "My bathtub," she said.

Lyanne giggled. "A bathtub?"

"It's deep, wide, and oval. Filled with bath oils and mounds of fluffy bubbles, it's pure heaven," Kris promised. "Showers just don't measure up to that kind of luxury."

"I never thought about it that way before," the girl said. "But at least I know what to give you as a present now."

Kris wrinkled her nose. "Not more taffy, I hope." Her mind went to those intoxicating chants concerning gifts for the favored, and the even more intoxicating gift Adam had given her when Lyanne was out of the room. "Besides, why would you want to give me something?"

"For helping Dean and the band," Lyanne insisted. "I'm a little sick of candy at the moment myself. I ate too much of it last night. But maybe you'd like to borrow my bathtub. Tomorrow you'll have the whole lodge to yourself. I'll be at school and Adam has to be in town for business and his doctor's appointment. You could use my bath salts and bubble bath, too."

Kris closed her eyes, savoring the promised treat. "It sounds heavenly. I accept."

*   *   *

The band hadn't been bad. They hadn't been that good, either, but with a little guidance Dean Taggart's group could be very passable. Kris and Lyanne had been invited to dinner with Dean's family after the rehearsal. Theirs was a large family full of friendly, boisterous children and adults. The Taggarts were more like a rerun of *The Waltons* than any family Kris had ever known. She found she liked the quiet pride in Dean's father's eyes and the gentle affection in Mrs. Taggart's face, especially when the woman was with Lyanne. The girl could do a lot worse than become part of the Taggart clan. If that was indeed what she wanted. It certainly appeared that Dean and his parents would welcome her when the time came.

At sixteen, Lyanne was still too young to be thinking of marriage, though. Her adolescent slang and her longing for wider shopping vistas alone were reasons to delay tying herself to any young man just yet. Judging by the few things she'd told Kris, it appeared that Lyanne wouldn't be averse to a glimpse of the bright lights. There had been too strong a hint of longing in her voice when she asked about New York.

Perhaps Adam Cheney was going at this problem from the wrong direction. Instead of getting Dean away from Lyanne, what he should be doing was taking his sister to the city. Any city.

Kris slept late the next morning. Once again she'd been up late reading more of the Klakith novels. It had become an addicting exercise now, rather than a tool to use in second-guessing Adam. When she woke, the clouds no longer hung low, skimming the ground. That morning there was no supernatural world to promise that dreams just might come true. The main lodge was unlocked but empty. A note dangled from the kitchen door inviting Kris to help herself to anything from coffee to Calgon bath beads. Kris interpreted that as carte blanche in Adam's office as well and placed her call to Los Angeles.

It didn't take as many strings as she'd feared to get Dean's band an interview with a booking agent. She must remember to tell them she'd changed the band's name, though. They'd chosen The Citadel. But that hadn't been snappy enough. She'd told the agent they were known as Dealer's Choice. After all, it had been at Adam's behest that the band was getting its step up in the music world. It was only fitting that their name be linked to the Klakith legends as well.

By the time she'd finished her calls and had coffee and leftover cinnamon rolls, it was early afternoon. With no reason to delay longer, Kris made her way up the stairs to her promised treat. She'd brought a small bag with her robe and a change of clothing along. At the top of the stairs she found Lyanne's room easily. It ran the length of the lodge and faced the back, the windows overlooking the same scene as that from the kitchen window. It was a more spectacular view from the second story. Meadow and forest stretched in a panorama that combined a freedom of space with the cozy sense of being sheltered from the rest of the world.

It was no surprise to find the room was a froth of pastels. A narrow white canopy bed held center stage, draped in a print of abstract yellow, pink, and blue flowers. Matching valances swept dramatically across twin dormer windows. The same fabric appeared on the window-seat cushions, as a dressing-table skirt, even as a curtain around the bathtub in the adjacent room.

Kris set her suitcase aside on a chair and leaned against the door molding, marveling at the wonders hidden away at Klakith Lodge. Lyanne's tub was painted a powder-puff blue. It was also long, deep, and fitted with claw feet. The sight of it was enough to make a woman weak. Kris lost no time filling the marvel with steaming water, perfume, and bubble bath. She didn't even mind that the latter was in a pink plastic bottle shaped like a seahorse.

It was pure decadent pleasure to sink into the mound of bubbles, to feel the warm, scented water close around her. Kris propped her feet on the rim of the tub, leaned back into the bath, and closed her eyes. Tensions seeped away. Her mind went fuzzy, refusing to dwell on anything other than the delicious sensation of water against her skin.

The mirror steamed up, as did the windows. Outside the world was overcast, cold, damp. In her private world, though, it was sensuous, warm, wet . . .

The water cooled all too soon. Reluctantly Kris stepped out and opened the drain. Her fair hair curled where it clung at her brow and at the nape of her neck. Her fingers and toes were pleasantly wrinkled from the long soak. Kris splashed on cologne and slipped into her long ivory robe. She wondered if Lyanne would mind if she warmed up this delightful way each day for the rest of her stay. How long a stay would it be? As eager as she'd been to end the assignment, Kris now found she was reluctant to finish.

It was much later than she'd thought, Kris found when she picked up her watch. Lyanne would be back from school at any moment. The girl had explained that she drove herself down to the high school each day in the Trooper. Once Adam had the use of his right leg again Lyanne would probably lose the freedom to drive herself everywhere. In the meantime, when Adam had to be somewhere, Luther B. had pitched in as chauffeur. Although Adam was being driven, sartorial elegance wasn't part of his handyman's service. Luther B.'s truck rivaled Dean Taggart's dilapidated Ford in both looks and noise. She'd have ample warning of his return.

The water gurgled out of the tub, but that was the only sound to disturb the peace at Klakith Lodge.

When Kris heard a footstep in the hall she knew her young hostess had returned home. A contented smile curved her lips as she tightened the belt on her robe and swept out of the room to meet the girl.

And came face-to-face with Adam.

sixteen

THEY STOOD STILL, EACH UNCERTAIN.

Kris thought he looked wonderful. Adam's thick red-earth hair was tousled from the wind. The raven's-wing color of his sweater only accented the broad width of his shoulders and chest. He wore snug corduroy slacks the color of desert sand, and black loafers.

Two shoes, not just one now. There were no crutches propped under his arms, only a cane. It swung jauntily back and forth on the doorknob of his room across the hall.

Adam took in Kris's deshabille. Her bare toes, the damp curls about her face. The faint blush that the heat of the bath had painted in her cheeks.

And the way the terry-cloth skirt of her robe parted as she moved, displaying her beautiful long legs.

Neither of them seemed to make the effort to close the distance, yet each took a fatal step.

The exotic scent of island blossoms surrounded Adam,

enhancing the moment with a fantasy-like aura. Frozen in time, he looked deep into the blue fathoms of Kris's eyes, watched them darken, swirl with primitive emotion. She swayed nearer, raised a bit on tiptoe as he loomed over her. Her mouth glistened as if touched by dew.

Kris's lips were parted and eager when they met his. Adam savored the taste of her, his mouth slanting hungrily over hers, bent on savoring the nectar she offered. And Kris responded as he had always known she would, with a need as primitive and compelling as his own. As if unaware of her state of undress, Kris pressed close to him, the soft curves of her tall form fitting perfectly against the hardness of his body. Oh, so perfectly. She was his Eve, made specifically for his pleasure alone.

As if mesmerized, Adam pulled the sash of her robe loose, slid his hands beneath the fabric to caress her rib cage, to cup her breast. He'd tried to imagine the texture of her in his dreams, had endeavored to transplant his fantasy to reality. Yet he'd failed. She was as soft as down. Beneath his fingertips Adam could feel the steady, increasingly wild tempo of Kris's heart. It fluttered as if it beat for him alone.

Perhaps it did at this preciously frozen moment. He was sure his own heart had stopped, afraid to find she was another figment of his imagination. But Kris breathed life back into him, made his blood hammer in his veins. Her body pressed against Adam's in an unconscious, wholly natural movement. Adam drew her closer still.

The touch of his hand against her newly heated flesh was like no sensation Kris had known before. It was an ache, poignant and insistent. More than the pleasant dizziness she'd felt when he'd caressed her face and kissed her before. So much more than the unknown power that had sent her into his arms that day on the staircase. Everything he did seemed so right. Every whimper she made so strange and new. She'd had lovers before. Their caresses had left her cold. But Adam . . . His name alone sang in her blood. How apt that he should be the one to make her being hum with life.

Was this feeling what caused her mother to run from one man to another, searching? This mindless longing, this feeling of both power and helplessness?

She could no longer resist Adam. Didn't want to resist. Didn't want to think. All she wanted to do was stay in his arms. And yet, even that ecstasy wasn't enough.

Adam's lips caressed, savored. His touch had her quivering beneath his hands. Like a famished man, his mouth explored her face, savored the elegant length of her throat. The robe was falling from her shoulders, slipping away like a whisper, an echo of her own forgotten determination to meet him only in battle. Surrender was preferable. Not only her surrender to her emotions, to him, but Adam's to her.

And then the front door of the lodge opened.

The sound shocked Adam back to a realization of where they were, of the too-real chance of being discovered by his sister.

Kris's mind was still hazy with pleasure, but his reflexes were excellent. Before she could catch a ragged breath, he'd pushed her back inside Lyanne's room and closed the door.

Still disoriented, Kris leaned against the wood weakly. He was gone. He'd left her, left her wanting. Hurting. Her robe hung open. Her skin was still on fire where Adam's hands had caressed her. She knew he'd been as caught up as she. Passion had flared as brightly, as violently as an erupting volcano. Like lava, it had flowed in a burning, consuming path that touched her mind as well as her body.

And Adam had put her aside. Had closed the door between them with a firmness that seemed to belie the molten heat in his golden eyes.

She could hear his step in the hall, hesitant as he limped slowly down the stairs, answering his sister's eager welcome.

The trill of Lyanne's cheerful chatter was like a bucket of cold water. It washed over Kris, bringing with it a horrified realization of what she'd just done. How much she'd given of herself.

Yet she'd known it would happen. Deep within her something had told Kris that first day that Adam Cheney was not a man she could ignore. Or forget. That he alone held a key to a lock she hadn't even realized existed.

She took a few deep breaths, hoping that they would calm her. By the time Lyanne came up the stairs, Kris was dressed and in control once more.

But for how long? she wondered.

They were all seated in the kitchen. It was the room that the Cheneys seemed to gravitate to naturally. Kris found that after a scant three days with them, she'd picked up the habit herself.

Lyanne was munching on an apple. She'd worn narrow-legged jeans to school that day, cowboy boots, and a high-necked sweater that featured a decoration of dangling rawhide strips. Her long hair was pulled to one side in a ponytail that wagged just behind her left ear.

Adam sat across from his sister, absently rubbing the knee of his newly freed leg. He leaned a bit heavily on his cane when he got up, but any offer of assistance from either Lyanne or Kris was met with a scowl. He'd been dependent for too long, and found simple pleasure in the refound ability to help himself.

Kris accepted a cup of coffee but barely touched it. Part of her still ached with longing. Part of her raged at the mindless way she'd gone into his arms again. Once, when Lyanne's back was turned, Kris met Adam's eyes. And felt seared by his touch once more.

The sweet scent of the apple flavored the air. It made Kris's mouth water, although she couldn't say why she was suddenly hungry. She must have looked famished, for Adam pushed the bowl of rosy fruit across the table toward her.

That was a switch, Kris thought, as she chose a piece. Adam offering his Eve an apple. Lord, he did make her feel like Eve. Like she was the only woman who existed—the only one who mattered. Which, of course, she wasn't. His gaze had already turned to the one he'd catered to for ten long years. His sister.

The first bite Kris took of the apple was wonderful. It was as if her taste buds had been enhanced. The fruit tasted more poignant, more refreshing. Her senses seemed heightened. She fancied she could hear the air itself move. Could see new shadings in colors. Everything seemed so much brighter.

Or perhaps it was merely that she felt so much more alive. So aware of things. Particularly, of Adam Cheney.

Kris took another bite of her apple, felt the juice trickle at the corner of her mouth. Felt Adam's wolf gaze drink in the way it coursed toward her chin before being retrieved by a flick of her tongue. She felt exotic and decadent. And so wonderful.

He played with the handle of his coffee mug, his index finger stroking along the smooth curve. Kris watched, her mind replaying the feel of his hand, faintly callused and masculinely rough, as it had caressed her not long before.

"I stopped by the doctor's office before coming home,"

Lyanne announced between bites of her apple.

"Didn't trust me to tell you what he said, huh," Adam said.

The teenager giggled. "Of course not. You never do."

"Most of what he said is self-evident. It will take time to get rid of the limp, but I'll heal," he said.

"Ha!" Lyanne looked decidedly superior. "He told me you need physical therapy. Not just walking, but a regular, guided session with a therapist."

"Can't be done."

Lyanne nodded. "Not in Cedar City. But in Vegas . . ."

"Doc already knows my feelings on that," Adam growled.

The girl bit into her apple again. "I told him you'd go."

Adam's expression was thunderous, but his voice was carefully level. "There's too much to do here," he said. "You've got two months of school yet. I've got a deadline on the last book to meet. If he'd suggested it a couple months down the line, I'd agree. But as it is . . ."

His sister wasn't giving in, though. Kris watched the stubborn set of Lyanne's jaw grow more determined. She wondered if Adam realized how much the girl resembled him when she got that resolute look on her face.

"That's too late, Adam. The damage will be done. I don't want you stuck with a limp because you're too pigheaded to leave the lodge," Lyanne insisted.

"I can't leave."

"Can," she countered. "I can stay with Becky's family."

"We aren't imposing on them indefinitely."

"It's just for the rest of the school year."

"I said no."

"Adam." Lyanne's snarl was insistent.

He was just as emphatic. "No."

Kris savored her apple and watched the pair. "Perhaps I might make a suggestion?"

Two pair of golden eyes turned on her, one eager, one a bit malevolent.

"Why don't you both go to Las Vegas?" Kris asked.

Adam turned his attention back to his coffee mug, finding the grain of the stoneware worthy of an angry glare. "Out of the question."

Lyanne's eyes glowed with an excited light, like finely cut and faceted topaz.

Kris didn't think the battle could be won as long as the girl was in the room, though. She needed to explain her reasoning to Adam without such an eager audience.

"I called LA earlier," Kris said, changing the subject. "I can't guarantee that Dean's group will be taken on by this guy, but here's the number of the agent I talked to about them." She handed Lyanne the scrap of paper on which she'd scribbled notes.

The girl bounded to her feet immediately. "That's wonderful!" she cried, and surprised Kris by giving her an enthusiastic hug. "I've got to call Dean!" She glanced down at the paper. "What's Dealer's Choice mean? It's not the title of one of the Klakith books."

"Ah . . . er . . . it's the band's new name," Kris explained uneasily.

"Oh." Lyanne accepted the alteration without a question and dashed from the room.

Adam's stormy look had cleared, Kris was relieved to see. Unfortunately, she was sure it would return soon.

"Dealer's Choice?" he said.

"It seemed . . . er . . . apt." Kris put the core of her apple aside on a napkin. She didn't meet his eyes when she spoke, but fiddled with the edge of the cloth. "Adam, I think you should go to Las Vegas."

When Kris glanced up, she found he was studying his coffee mug once more.

"Because of the limp?" he asked.

"Because the therapy is needed," Kris said. "But more importantly, because it is an excellent excuse to use for a move to a big city."

"First step of the tour?" He was hostile now. "You haven't got Taggart out of the way yet, slick."

His tone infuriated her. They'd been so close, so totally in tune during the insane minutes in each other's arms. Now he seemed to forget that intimacy, to put them back on opposite sides of a battlefield.

"Lord! Does your mind ever get off that track?" Kris spat. "You wanted me to make friends with Lyanne. Well, I think I have. And she's told me some things you probably don't even know."

His feral glance was centered on her now. It did strange and wonderful things to her. "Like what?" he asked suspiciously.

"She's curious about the city. Not Las Vegas per se. Any city."

"And?"

Kris took a deep breath and leaned forward. Who knew how long Lyanne would be gone? She had to convince him quickly before the chance was lost.

"Listen. There's a good chance of the band getting a few gigs out of my contact in LA. But why let Lyanne sit here at home, where she can visit the rest of the Taggarts, see Dean's friends? Be constantly reminded of him? I'm getting him temporarily out of the way. Get Lyanne out of the area while you've got the chance. Show her a taste of what life can be like outside of the mountains. Let her meet more people. More young men. Give her something to compare her current life against."

Adam didn't look convinced. But he didn't refuse to consider it.

"You really think that would work?" he asked at last.

"Can't hurt."

He studied her intent expression a moment longer. "All right," he said, his voice suddenly weary. "We'll move to Vegas."

seventeen

KRIS LEFT KLAKITH LODGE THE NEXT DAY. SHE'D BEEN
delegated by a taciturn Adam to find a house, a high school,
and a physical therapist. He'd had more specifications concerning the school than anything else. Lyanne's enthusiasm
was for the type of dwelling. She wanted it to have a
swimming pool.

Kris had left the mountain bundled in her fur, but by the
time she pulled into Las Vegas she had shed it and her
sweater. April had barely burst, but in the desert valley the
temperatures were already stretching toward summer. There
was no doubt that Lyanne would get Adam's money's worth
out of a pool in the coming months.

Although she was used to working with other people's
expense accounts, it felt very strange to have Adam's bank
draft in her pocket. The amount seemed astronomical, but
Kris knew that she'd have exhausted the funds long before
she returned to Cedar City.

He'd given her a week. Kris planned to be gone less. The drive to Las Vegas had taken only a couple hours but she missed him already.

Amazing that she should feel this way about someone who'd been just a name to her the week before. It wasn't just the way Adam made her feel when he touched her, or kissed her. Kris was enchanted with the way he wrote, with the characters he created. She was amazed that he had taken on the responsibility of raising his sister at such a young age. At the excellent job he'd done with Lyanne.

Although Adam felt the girl had gotten out of hand, Kris was sure that he had nothing to worry about. Lyanne, for all her girlish silliness, had a level head on her shoulders. Kris doubted the teenager would ever do anything to disappoint her brother. Their visible affection was extraordinary in a world where siblings and parents often were too busy or too self-absorbed to spend time together.

What Adam saw as signs that he was losing his sister, Kris saw as evidence that Lyanne was growing up. Not because a certain number of years had passed by, but because, for once, her brother had been dependent on *her*.

Now that Adam's cast was off, the tensions would come to the fore. In being the family errand runner, Lyanne had tasted a freedom that Adam resented. Would he accept the change? Or would he fight against it?

And would Kris end up in the middle of the battlefield?

Kris put the thoughts aside, checked into Bally's on the Las Vegas Strip, and proceeded to while the night away with dreams of Adam.

Next morning she was at the real estate office early. Her requirements were so specific, there were only a few rental properties available for her choice. By noon she'd surprised the agent by taking a four-bedroom, three-bath ranch-style house complete with kidney-shaped pool, Jacuzzi, and three-car garage. Pleased with her success, Kris celebrated by shopping at the Fashion Show Mall across from the tall, gold-tinted facade of the Mirage Hotel and Casino.

The next day wasn't as easy. She wished Belinda was with her. Decorating a home had never come within Kris's range of assignments before. It wasn't as if she were buying furnishings. Everything from drapes to sofas to bedroom suites would be temporary. By evening she had a headache, but the house would be habitable within two days. Adam's bank account was greatly depleted, but the size of the bites she put in it ensured immediate service.

On day three Kris wound down. Utilities were turned on. She visited Bonanza High School, paving the way for Lyanne's entrance the following week. She scouted out a health club and arranged for Adam's physical therapy. Then, her thoughts on Lyanne's mobility, Kris added one final chore to her list. She rented the girl a car.

That night Kris felt drained when she called the lodge to report the extent of her success. Lyanne was agog over the idea of having both a swimming pool and a car of her own to drive. She was so thrilled she nearly forgot to pass along some information of her own. Dean Taggart and his band had gone to Los Angeles at the behest of the booking agent.

It wasn't Lyanne's news that warmed Kris, though. It was Adam's deep voice.

"Not a bad start, slick," he admitted when Lyanne relinquished the phone.

He made her feel short of breath. "Glad to be of service," she said.

Adam laughed. "Ah, now that's another subject. One that's been preying on my mind of late."

Kris felt as if his hand had just skimmed over her, his touch warm, insistent, possessive. "Has it really?"

"Constantly," he murmured.

"Mine too," she said in a husky whisper.

Adam's voice was as vibrant and low as the purr of a contented panther. "Being one of those thoroughly boring guys who methodically plots his actions," he said, "I put my mind to solving that little problem."

Kris held her breath. "You mean . . . ah . . . time together?"

"Without you-know-who." He paused a moment.

Kris was sure he could hear the way her breath had quickened, how her heart hammered.

"When will you be back?" Adam asked.

There was still the delivery of the furniture to oversee but she couldn't wait much longer. "I'll be home tomorrow night," Kris said.

Home.

She hadn't realized she'd said that word until after Adam hung up. How much had her life changed? She never would have believed this illogical twist of fate if a psychic had forecast it. But it was true. Home was no longer her apartment back in Manhattan. It was a cabin on top of a mountain in Utah.

All because she was in love.

When had she stopped fearing the fall? Where had the turning point been? Had it been when she and Adam had shared those passion-filled moments? Had it been when he agreed to move to Las Vegas, even temporarily? Or had she fallen hopelessly in love just moments ago when she'd heard the tender rumble of his voice on the phone?

Did it matter? She'd known the man barely a week. They'd growled at each other from the first day. Kris doubted that they'd ever stop being on opposite sides of some fences. They were both just too used to getting their own way.

But she loved him. Just the thought of soon being able to consummate that love gave her chills. And another wonderfully sleepless night.

The sun had set behind her hours ago. Kris had watched the last rays from the back patio of the house in Las Vegas. They had created a pallet in the sky of pink, then purple, before disappearing behind the Spring Mountain range.

She loved the outlook from the house. The view stretched for miles, nearly unsullied by civilization. Perhaps half-a-dozen other homes faced the house across a stretch of man-made lake. But if you ignored them, which Kris found easy to do, the vista was of blue water, endless sky, and steeply rising mountains. The latter were splashed with various shades of gray, white, and tones of red. She thought Adam would like that aspect. It reminded her faintly of the descriptions he'd written of the planet Klakith.

Before she left, Kris took one last tour of the house, dawdling from room to room. The living room was a bit formal. The walls were roughly textured with heavily laid-on swirls of eggshell paint. The color was repeated in the deep pile of the carpet and the seven-foot sofa and twin Queen Anne wing chairs. She'd arranged them to face each other over a bleached-wood coffee table. A dried flower arrangement nearly five feet tall gave the room a touch of color with cool blues and greens that picked up the tints of water, sky, and the patch of grass that served as a lawn out front.

The main room was separated from a family room/kitchen area by a gracefully curved archway. Here the flooring imitated nature in a flat dull slate. She'd followed the decorator's lead and chosen couches in a plush mist tone, highlighting them with toss pillows of eggshell, blue, and green. A textile of rough wools hung on the wall. Shelves displayed the aqua stoneware Kris had bought, and the gently shaded matching crystal.

The extra bedroom would serve as Adam's office. Here the furniture was gunmetal gray. An IBM personal computer, laser printer, fax machine, and copier awaited him. All Adam would have to pack were his diskettes.

The room that would be hers was simply furnished. As a guest she hadn't felt right in choosing anything too extravagant. Here an imitation-brass bedstead and modest pine dresser were the sole furnishings. She'd indulged in a vibrant set of sheets and matching spread with a sky-blue design. A trail of ivy tendrils curled across the dresser top but the silk plant was the only accessory she'd added.

Lyanne's room reflected her private setting back at Klakith Lodge. Kris had replaced the narrow canopy bed with a queen-sized mattress and natural wicker headboard. The other furnishings were also of wicker, including a Victorian lounger piled high with toss pillows. Plants hung from the ceiling and were reflected in a large oval mirror on a stand near the wardrobe. The bedspread was accented with ruffles of old lace against a pattern of sprigged lavender. The reverse side was a green stripe, as were the ruffles around the flowered bolsters. Kris had been generous with the pillows, creating a pile that she hoped would urge Lyanne to curl up for long chats with new friends using the elegant French-styled telephone on the nightstand.

The room she'd agonized over was the master suite. In the end she'd chosen classic styling. As in the rest of the house, the carpeting was a thick cream. To offset it, Kris had picked dark mahogany furniture. The room was large enough to offer a separate sitting room and she had used deep chocolate leather chairs, one with a matching footstool, to give Adam a private place to relax. The bed coverings were a deep maroon, some pin-striped, some solid. She'd found a richly textured Indian rug to hang on the wall but didn't feel it really reflected Adam's personality. It would have to do, though.

Kris closed the front door softly and soon had turned the BMW toward the east once more, heading it back toward Utah. She was pleased with her efforts, but nervous about what Adam and Lyanne would think of them.

Or perhaps it was the thought of spending time alone with Adam that made her nervous. He'd plotted a way for them to take up where Lyanne's return had interrupted them.

Would it be as . . .

Kris's mind stalled.

Would he . . .

Her mouth was dry. Her imagination refused to go beyond the delicious sensations of that spontaneous afternoon when she'd gone blindly into his arms.

He'd planned, Adam had said. Well, so had she. Her shopping spree at the mall had been to equip her with ammunition. Like the new negligee in her suitcase. It wasn't black, but a transparent Normass white.

Lord! What was wrong with her? Never before had she been this highstrung over a man. She'd actually sneered at other women who'd acted this way. Had never been able to understand what made them so anxious. But she was anxious. Afraid that she wouldn't be able to live up to his expectations, to his fantasies.

When the time came, would she be his Emling? Or would Adam be willing to make do with just Kris, with all her faults and insecurities?

She passed the bright lights of the resort in Mesquite, Nevada, and wound her way through the spectacular walls of the Virgin River Gorge without consciously knowing time was passing. St. George, Utah, fell behind, and all too soon the turn into the Dixie National Forest was before her.

Adam had been pacing for nearly an hour, leaning heavily on his cane, yet nearly unaware of the pain in his knee. He threw more wood on the fire, watched the sparks spray like a firework display on the Fourth of July. Looked at his watch. Looked at it again a few minutes later.

Where had he ever gotten the idea that precise planning was the ideal way to run his life? All those hours spent dreaming about what he'd do if he was alone with Kris Jackson! Wasted! He was too worked up to sit still, too nervous to think straight.

Lyanne had driven off to her friend Becky's house hours ago, leaving him alone with his anxieties. She would be staying overnight with Becky's family, who would drive Lyanne to Las Vegas tomorrow, their eldest son at the wheel of Adam's Trooper. His leg could handle driving for short stints, but not the hours it would take to reach the city. Since Lyanne and Becky had been tearful at their impending separation, it had been easy to maneuver the two teens into pleading for one more night together. Adam had known that Becky's family would volunteer to help with the move. All he had to do was guide the direction he wanted everyone to run.

In the morning he'd go to Las Vegas with Kris. Lyanne and her entourage would appear in time for dinner. He'd promised to take them all out to eat at the Circus Circus Buffet. The youngsters would run wild on the Midway while the adults pumped a few coins into slot machines. Then the visitors would drive back to Utah and he would return to his new home. The one Kris Jackson had chosen for him.

He'd thought about what she'd said, that in getting Lyanne away from the mountain he would be opening his sister to new vistas. At least he'd tried to think about it. There had been so much to do since he'd agreed to the move. Lyanne's school had been consulted, her records gathered for transfer to Las Vegas. Luther B. had been contacted to move onto the lodge property. He'd chosen one of the small cabins to live in rather than move into the Cheneys' home. There had been calls to New York reporting the change of address to Asteroid Books. And a very surprising session at the bank. He'd arranged to transfer funds to the nearest First Interstate branch in Nevada, and tried not to dwell on the state of his account. In between it all, he'd tried to work.

Within a short time the set pace of his life had become hectic. All because of one woman.

Part of him insisted that the move was in Lyanne's interests. But late at night when he couldn't sleep, Adam knew he'd capitulated because Kris had asked it of him. If she hadn't come to Klakith Lodge, life would have gone on as it had every day for the last six years. Lyanne would go to school, see her friends, and either argue or tease over dinner. He would write, fish, and wonder what the future would bring.

It had brought Kris Jackson. And he wasn't ready to deal with the future she now thrust upon him.

Oh, it wasn't the idea of enduring a brief promotional tour that bothered him. He'd known the day would come when he'd no longer be able to hide behind the mystery of Roidan Ryder. He'd merely hoped to stave it off a few years longer.

But Kris wouldn't allow him to coast any longer. Just her presence made him consider his own future. It didn't matter whether Lyanne left him to go to college or replaced him with a husband and family of her own. One way or another he would be alone. The propulsion that had driven him for ten long years would be gone.

Once he'd fancied himself in love. But the woman of his choice had turned away, preferring to be free, to start a family in her own time, not become part of a ready-made nucleus. He could understand that. Or thought he could. But Lyanne was too much a part of him to shrug off his responsibility for her. If a woman couldn't accept his sister, couldn't care for her as much as he did, there was no future that he could share with her. That had been how it was when Maggie had left him. It would be the same with Kris.

Kris.

Adam sat on the edge of the settee and stared into the blazing fire. He rubbed his knee. It was almost a reflex to do so now.

Perhaps he was a fool to even attempt to woo her. For that was what he was doing. Some would call it seduction, this careful maneuvering to be alone with her. One night wasn't enough, though. Or even a series of nights. He wanted a lifetime.

Adam looked at his watch again, wondered when Kris had left Las Vegas, where she was at that moment. If she was thinking of him.

eighteen

KRIS THOUGHT OF LITTLE ELSE BUT ADAM CHENEY ALL day. Although he hadn't actually told her, she knew that Lyanne would be gone when she arrived at the lodge. Before leaving the house in Las Vegas, Kris had gone to trouble with her appearance. But when she pulled off the main road and into the Klakith compound, the insecurities plagued her once more.

What if she'd read him wrong? What if Lyanne was at home?

What if she wasn't?

Kris had always been too tall, too thin, too bossy for other men. When Adam really got to know her, the affair they were about to begin would be as doomed as all the others in her past. Realizing the outcome ahead of time wouldn't temper the hurt, or minimize it. If she were smart, she'd turn the BMW around and head down the mountain. She'd avoid the chance of intimacy, the chance of getting hurt.

The only lights at Klakith came from the main lodge. They were soft, coaxing. The gentle glow warmed the windows of the main room. The office itself was dark. But above it, the wide windows that faced the lake spilled subdued light from Adam's bedroom.

Kris swallowed loudly. She gathered her courage. She was the woman who'd faced down drunken actors, peevish poets, and lecherous rock and rollers. One handsome hermit would not best her.

She pulled the BMW to a stop before the main building. She tilted the rearview mirror, checked her hair, licked at her suddenly dry lips. The collar of her coat was pulled high. The fur tickled the lobes of her ears, caressed the long, bare expanse of her throat. Kris fingered her diamond earring studs. Pinched her pale cheeks. Chewed on her bottom lip once more. Then stepped out of the car.

The temperature in Las Vegas had been in the seventies that afternoon, but here on the mountain, with the sunset past, it was freezing. The mud crunched beneath Kris's shoes. The wooden planks of the steps creaked beneath her step.

For the first time since she'd arrived, Kris knocked on the broad front door.

There was a welcoming bark from Honey, the Irish setter, just before it opened. The dog scuttled out, circled Kris excitedly, eagerly sniffing her feet. The hound's feathered tail whipped back and forth through the cold air, wagging in ecstasy. Finding herself ignored, the dog soon gave up and returned inside. Her nails rang against the polished wood floor as she padded across the room to curl up on the rug before the fire.

Kris was barely conscious of the animal. She tugged nervously at the collar of her coat.

He was silhouetted against the light. Tall, broad. A giant

who made her feel small and delicate.

"Hi," Kris said. Her breath came out in a cloud of vapor.

"Welcome back." Adam held the door wide, stepped back so that she could sweep past him. "How was the drive?"

He closed the door, stood over her.

"Long," she murmured. Or had it been too short? Was she really ready yet? She'd dreamed of the night to come. Agonized over it.

Adam's smile was warm. He wasn't pushing her. In fact, he seemed as anxious as Kris to draw the moment out.

He'd dressed nearly as formally as she had. His three-piece suit was a navy pinstripe. His shirt alternated white-and-blue stripes. His silk tie was slashes of red against a navy background.

"Let me take your coat," Adam suggested. He moved just behind her. His hands touched her shoulders.

"All right." Kris's voice was soft and strained with tension. She sounded frightened. But it was excitement that fluttered wildly inside her, beating its wings against her rib cage, making her short of breath.

Adam inhaled the exotic scent of her perfume. It befuddled his senses, left him a bit mesmerized.

The fur slipped from her shoulders, revealing first the tempting curve of her neck and the narrow diamond necklace that rested against her collarbone, its center stone nestled in the hollow of her throat. Small stones dazzled at her ears, peeping from the feathery arrangement of her champagne-pale hair. Her shoulders were nearly bare, her neckline scooped low.

Slowly Adam let his eyes savor the sight. The glow of black satin against her faintly blushing skin, the arch of her foot in a high-heeled shoe, the erotic view of long shapely legs in black stockings.

Kris's eyes were dark as the night. They glistened like the distant stars when she turned her face up to his. "Will I do?" she asked.

He skimmed over the simple slip dress, lingering at the narrow straps, savoring their dark glow against her white skin. "You'll do just fine," Adam murmured and turned away to put her coat in the closet. "Have you eaten?"

Kris shook her head. She hadn't been able to think about food all day. But the cozy smell of burning wood in the fireplace was being overridden by the tempting aromas of Italy. "Smells like . . ." She paused, wondering what Lyanne might have thrown together before leaving.

"Chicken cacciatore. One of my specialties," he said.

Her eyes widened. He hadn't thought they could grow so big, could look so startled.

Adam laughed. "Who do you think did the cooking for this family the last ten years? Lye's only tried her hand this last year. My repertoire is wider." He led the way to the kitchen, his limp a bit more pronounced than he would have liked. He was damned if he'd use the cane that night. He hoped he didn't look as decrepit as the pain in his knee made him feel.

"I'm sorry the surroundings aren't as plush as I would have liked tonight," Adam apologized, pushing the swinging door open for Kris. "I'll do better next time."

Next time. Her heart swelled.

The setting couldn't have been more perfect as far as Kris was concerned. It didn't matter that there were no violinists standing by to serenade them. It didn't matter that the dinnerware was made by Corelle, or that there was no bridal-white linen tablecloth.

The table was set for two. Only the soft, intimate glow of a single hurricane lamp illuminated it. She hadn't noticed before, but rather than the usual loud jarring chords of rock and roll, a mellow jazz piano played in the background.

Adam pulled her chair out for her, hovered a moment as if he were considering whether to kiss the temptingly exposed nape of her neck. Then he pulled out the adjacent chair and joined her at the table.

A chafing dish had kept the meal warm. Adam served Kris, then himself. He poured red wine into delicately stemmed goblets.

"Shall we have a toast?" he asked.

Kris raised her glass. "Certainly. What to?"

A lazy smile played at the corners of his mouth, lit his golden wolf eyes. "To Starburst Pictures and Asteroid Books," he said, surprising Kris. "For sending you to me."

There was a definite lump in her throat now. "For sending me to you," she agreed in a whisper and washed the constriction away with wine.

"Hell," Adam said. He put his wineglass down, leaned toward her. His large hands cupped her face, his fingers gliding along Kris's downy cheeks before sliding into the short, soft sweep of her hair.

"I missed you," he murmured and brushed her lips with his in a tentative kiss.

From there it was easy. The intensity of the caress increased, grew warmer, more insistent.

Kris leaned toward him. He tasted of wine. "I missed you, too," she said against his mouth. "Lord, I missed you."

The food cooled on their plates, forgotten. "I want you," Adam whispered. "Have since the first day when you stood over me hissing like a cat."

"I don't hiss," Kris said, but her voice was as soft and mesmerized as his. Her fingers were entangled in his hair. But there was still too much space between them. She flowed from her chair and into his lap, her lips never leaving his.

Adam groaned a bit, deep in his throat.

"Am I hurting your leg?" she asked, immediately contrite and poised for flight.

The pain was persistent but miniscule compared to the way his other senses hammered. Adam's arm tightened around her waist. His hand slid up her thigh. "Do I look like I'm suffering?" he asked in a teasing voice.

Kris smiled tenderly. "No, I suppose not."

He shifted her to a more intimate position. "At least not with my bum leg," Adam said.

"So I can tell."

They gazed into each other's eyes a moment.

"We should eat," he suggested.

"Are you hungry?"

His voice was a deep, tender rumble. "For you."

Kris felt breathless again.

"I wish I could carry you to bed," Adam said. "But do you think you could walk there just this once?"

Her footsteps lagged, waiting for him to make his way slowly up the stairs. She'd brought the wine goblets. Adam carried the bottle. His limp was more pronounced than it had been when she'd left the lodge earlier in the week. Although he tried to disguise it, she read pain in his eyes with each tortured step he took. It was pride that kept Adam going. Pride that left his cane hanging on the back of a settee in the living room.

Kris bit her lip to keep from reminding him that only days before his leg had been in a protective cast. Tomorrow she'd nag. Tonight . . . Tonight she'd make sure he was enchanted enough not to mind her nagging.

The door to Lyanne's room stood open, but Adam's was

closed. Kris waited outside. She thought the lines around his mouth were more pronounced when he reached the top of the stairs, but his bearing was straight and sure. If he breathed a bit heavily, well, she did, too. In anticipation.

Adam reached past Kris and pushed the door open.

The day she'd been alone in the house Kris had been tempted to peek inside Adam's domain. She'd resisted, telling herself that such an invasion would be prying, would make her little better than a Peeping Thomasina. Now she was glad she had waited.

It was a very masculine lair. Yet there was nothing stark or Spartan about the furnishings. They were lush, dark, sensuous.

But it was the view that drew Kris. It stretched in a panorama across the length of the room, a display of stars so vast, it made her breathless. The night sky sparkled with diamond-bright lights. Galaxies seemed laid out just for her pleasure. And beneath them, the lake moved restlessly, its waters reflecting the sparkling firmament. And around the edges of the shoreline, mountain pines thrust upward as if the top branches were trying to touch each star.

She knew now why Lyanne had said these windows commanded the best view.

"Oh, Adam," Kris whispered. "It's beautiful."

"The view? Yes, it is," he said, but he was looking only at her.

Kris blushed with pleasure and stepped into the room.

The lighting was muted. A thick carpet hushed their footsteps. Its Armenian design was worked in deep jewel tones, reds, greens, blues, golds. The same figures and colors were almost duplicated in the exotic spread that covered a king-sized bed.

Adam surprised her by avoiding the bed. Instead he limped over to the hearth, bent to a basket of wood, and threw fresh kindling on the fire. When the blaze was licking happily at a new selection of logs, he tossed pillows down on the floor before it.

Kris sank to her knees among them. Adam eased himself down next to her, cosseting his right leg. He refilled their wineglasses, toasted her silently and finished his quickly.

She followed his lead. Adam took the glass from her, set it aside. He tilted her face to his, a forefinger beneath Kris's chin, before kissing her once again.

He was lazily thorough. Content to take his time to explore all the avenues of pleasure with her. Kris wondered at his patience. Didn't he feel the same urgency that had built within her? It beat at her, demanding immediate release. But Adam's slow savoring of her lips held it at bay.

The same need was inside him. It flared in his eyes. Yet he forestalled it, in no hurry to finish. Just as the flames licked at the wood in the fireplace, the desire in his golden eyes touched her with a heat that left a mark. She felt scorched, branded by that look. And so very small and feminine.

Adam's hands cupped her face once more, then slid across her shoulders. Kris felt the delicate narrow straps of her dress give, gliding down off her shoulders. The zipper slid open down her back. Her bodice gaped, dropped lower, and Adam's lips now continued the exploration his fingers had begun.

Kris knelt, rising above Adam. She shrugged from the loosened bodice, letting the gown drop to her hips. Beneath it she wore a black lace corset. With Adam's help, her dress was soon draped casually across a side chair. Her hands slid across his chest, released each button of his waistcoat. Adam stripped both jacket and vest off in one motion, tossing them across the room. He tugged at his tie.

Kris pushed him back against the pillows, hovered over him, clad only in the exotic lingerie she'd bought in Las Vegas. For all her talk about spontaneity, Kris had done as much planning for this evening as Adam. Now her mouth slanted hungrily across his, savoring, teasing him. Her hands worked his tie loose, worked patiently at each button of his shirt. It was soon thrown aside as well.

The firelight gave her skin a warm golden glow. He was mesmerized by the sight of it, by the pale mounds of her breasts as they strained against the lace and ribbons on her camisole.

The feminine frills had been a jolt to his system. Although he'd seen the picture of Kris in the short, tight skirt in the magazine, had viewed the long stretch of her legs encased in form-fitting leather boots, her taste in apparel on the whole had leaned more toward the conservative. The tones she chose were neutral, grays, browns, various shades of beige. The coloring and cut had been subdued. She had no need of bright colors to draw attention to herself. Had never needed to point out the fact that she was extremely feminine.

Yet here she was in opaque lace and ribbons, donned, Adam was sure, to impress him.

As if she needed to. He'd been intoxicated with her from the start. He'd thought it was due to her resemblance to Emling. But it hadn't been. Reality far exceeded even his wildest dreams. While Emling would do for Dalwulf, only Kris Jackson would do for Adam Cheney.

Adam tugged gently on the straining ribbons. Kris's breasts spilled free. Framed by frothing lace, the small perfect mounds responded instantly to his touch.

He twisted, pulling her with him till she was sprawled beneath him. His mouth was hot, warm, wet against her skin. Kris arched with pleasure as Adam's tongue traced paths across her breast, then suddenly across her abdomen.

His hands and mouth moved ever lower, stripping away the fragile cloth that hid her from his view.

Her fingers slid through the dark curls on his chest, explored the tensing muscles across his back. In response to his touch, she raised herself toward him.

Adam took the invitation. His breath was labored. He poised between her welcoming thighs, his teeth clenched. Then he collapsed next to Kris, one hand going quickly to his right knee.

Kris watched him for a long silent moment. She should have known. His recent injury was still unwilling to accept his weight for any length of time. And Adam had already stretched it to the limit by refusing to use his cane that evening.

She leaned over, kissed his damp brow. Kissed his tightly closed eyes.

"Kris," he said, his voice a tight waver.

"Hush." Her lips moved across his face, brushed his mouth. Her hands slid as well. First over his chest, then lower, following the trail of dark hair to his groin. Yet on she moved, until her fingers rested on the center of his pain. Slowly, Kris massaged Adam's knee until she'd eased the tense muscles of his leg.

"Better?" she purred.

His breathing was normal once more. Or at least normal for a man with a nearly naked woman bent over him. "Much," he said. "I'm sorry, slick."

Kris chuckled softly. "Sorry? You're not finished yet, Dealer," she murmured. She slid over him, straddling him. "Think you can take things from here?"

Adam's teeth flashed in a wicked grin. His hands slid up her thighs and positioned themselves on her hips. "I just might," he said.

nineteen

IT WAS DIFFICULT TO GET OUT OF BED THE NEXT MORNING. Not only was it much warmer beneath the pile of blankets, but Kris and Adam were loath to end their idyll. Neither had slept much. Used to sleeping alone, each found the movements of the other made sleep impossible. Staying awake together was so much nicer anyway.

The Irish setter had joined them sometime during the night, curling up in her accustomed place at the foot of the bed. By dawn she'd decided the hearth was a more comfortable resting place. It wasn't as prone to bouncing as was Adam's wide bed that night.

By noon they were on the road. Kris was behind the wheel of the BMW. Adam had pushed the passenger's seat back as far as it would go to accommodate his long legs. He frequently rubbed his knee but it seemed more a reflex action than an attempt to ease pain. The Irish setter had curled up in the back seat and gone to sleep almost before they were past the rustic gates of Klakith Lodge.

Neither Kris nor Adam talked much. They exchanged frequent smiles. But the only subject on their minds was one that didn't need to be aired. Once Lyanne arrived at the house in Las Vegas, the opportunity for them to make love would be gone again.

Something had changed, though: the way Kris saw things. She'd driven the route between Las Vegas and Cedar City three times in the last ten days. She'd viewed the same stretches of desert, the same vista of rising rock. She'd followed the stretch of Interstate 15, weaving past Zion National Park, through the hamlet of St. George with its bright white Mormon temple. She'd shot down the glorious canyon of the Virgin River, unaware of the colors in the rock, of the steeply cut gorge. She'd been blind to the ribbon of water that twisted through it, seemingly unimpressed that, over the ages, it had cut the pass.

Their route spilled out of Utah, through a sliver of Arizona before bursting forth into the Nevada desert. The Virgin River worked its way down to join the Colorado River and Lake Mead. Rather than follow the trickle of green landscape that bordered the stream, the interstate forged across the dry desert floor toward the refreshing springs at what the Spanish had called Las Vegas, the meadows.

There was nothing very pretty about the arid region through which they drove. Unless, of course, you were in love. Kris admitted to herself that such was her state of mind. But she would never tell Adam. Such a confession would be akin to relinquishing control of her own life. It would give him a power over her. So she kept the singing quietly locked in her heart. A feeling to be cherished, and later, mourned over.

Mountains thrust skyward all along the route. Adam pointed out the various layers, the stratification of eons of sediment, that had built the stark hills. They tilted, rearranged by seismic activity. Some were tinted red; others were bleached white as the man-made pavement.

The signs came fast as they sped closer to the city. Exits for Nellis Air Force Base, North Las Vegas, Casino Center, and the Strip whipped by and fell behind them. Kris switched to the expressway, Route 95, and skimmed across the top of Las Vegas, heading northwest. She exited at the far western edge of the city, at Rainbow Boulevard, easing with all the confidence of a native into the lane that would take her south.

The city was all around them now. Shopping centers hugged every corner. Streets were three lanes wide in either direction. Traffic, even on Sunday, was hectic.

"According to the real estate lady, this is the fastest growing side of town," Kris explained to Adam. "There's a large housing development for retired people called Summerlin still farther west. The expressway is being built out that way to hug the base of the mountains."

Adam watched the pace around him. He had visited the city a couple times a year, but had rarely left Las Vegas Boulevard, the Strip. On those excursions he'd cruised the casino tables, narrowed his choice down to various lovely visitors, then had sat down to charm them either at a Twenty-One table or among the banks of video poker machines. He'd made the women's vacations memorable, and they'd made it possible for him to return to the mountain a very relaxed man.

The pace off the Strip was different, though. It was the normal heartbeat of the city. People sped by en route to their jobs. Families ferried children to sport or church events. Everyone seemed bent on accomplishing errands in the least amount of time, dashing from one shopping center to another.

Quite different from Cedar City. Different from his early years in California. Absolutely foreign when compared to the country town back in Illinois where he'd grown up.

An ancient van cut in front of Kris. Adam gritted his teeth when she didn't slow, but simply insulted the other driver with a swift gesture. He hadn't realized how secluded he was up in his mountain retreat. How much culture shock would hit him.

Kris turned off the busy road at Sahara and headed out toward the mountains. In the distance he could make out the lovely shades of the formations in the heart of a canyon. The rocks blushed in hues of rust-red and orange-red. Like a touch of Klakith.

He wasn't as sure about the housing development when she reached it.

The Lakes was a high-rent district. Adam could tell that just by the make and model of the automobiles in the driveways. But the postage-sized green lawns were too artificial for his taste. Homes should reflect the landscape, to Adam's way of thinking. In this sunbaked desert, natural plants should have been used, not sturdy strains of grass from another climate zone.

The man-made lake irritated him, too. It was sculptured like a giant swimming pool. A breeze stirred the surface up, setting the water to dance in a gentle rhythm. Someone in a small sailboat was out on the bright blue surface. Adam squinted against the reflection of sun-washed, dancing whitecaps.

Kris was quiet, visibly apprehensive about her choice when she pulled the BMW to a stop in the driveway of a long, low, white stucco house. There was the requisite Lilliputian lawn and a harsh block wall bracketing three sides of the property. Adam didn't hate it on sight. After all, Kris had chosen it to please him. But he didn't actually like it either. He couldn't disappoint her, though.

"Looks fine, slick," he said. "Give me the grand tour."

Kris brightened immediately. He made noises of approval as she led him through the place, room by room. He dangled a hand in the water of the Jacuzzi, agreeing that the heat would be an excellent part of the therapy treatments his doctor insisted he needed. At least when Lyanne arrived, she would be honestly enthusiastic over the swimming pool.

The room he liked best was the one Kris had planned for his private use. Adam checked his watch and reluctantly relinquished the idea of making love again. They had barely two hours before his sister and Becky's family were due to arrive, and there was still one important side trip to make before then.

"It's all great," he told Kris. "You just forgot one thing."

Her pert, perfect face fell. She looked around the room, her gaze lingering on the bed before darting to each item of furniture. The bed was made up, its sheets matching the deep berry spread. Thick towels of a similar hue hung in the attached bath. "What did I forget?"

"Food," Adam said. "The refrigerator is nearly empty."

Kris looked relieved. "Oh, but I thought we were going out to eat tonight."

"We are. But that doesn't mean anything to teenagers, slick. They're like a compact swarm of locusts. They'll eat anything, at any time. And they're always hungry." He pulled her by the hand. "Come on. I'll show you my supermarket technique."

It wasn't a technique so much as an ability to fill a shopping cart to overflowing within a very short time. While Kris pushed the basket. Adam leaned heavily on his cane and dropped item after item into it. Cereals, breads, lunch meats, and soft drinks followed bacon, eggs, milk, and chocolate syrup. He strode down one aisle after another tossing things back to Kris as she dawdled behind in amazement. Having checked out the formal glassware Kris had purchased, Adam added tumblers, patiently explaining that watching Lyanne mix chocolate milk in Waterford crystal would probably turn his hair gray.

Forty-five minutes later they were on their way back to the house, the BMW's trunk filled with grocery bags. It took a full half hour to store everything away. By then Adam was rubbing his knee more frequently and Kris was feeling out of her depth.

The reaction of Lyanne and Becky to the house was all that Kris could have hoped. Becky's parents nodded encouragement but Kris had caught the dubious look the older woman gave the pale carpet. Kris wasn't sure how to respond to a question on how to keep the soft eggshell pile clean. The idea that it would need extra attention had never occurred to her. She ended up agreeing blankly to the suggestion that everyone remove their shoes as soon as they entered the house.

The girls went into ecstasy over Lyanne's new room, especially the idea that she had a phone of her own there. The shrill giggles continued out to the garage for the inspection of the sporty red Daihatsu Kris had rented for Lyanne's use.

It was Becky's father, with frequent glances at his watch, who got them all out the door and headed for the Strip. The line at the Circus Circus Buffet was long but the visitors from Utah took it in stride. They suggested that Adam get off his feet and left him at a Twenty-One table. Kris, however, was stuck in line. By the time they had made it to the front of the procession, Kris's smile was beginning to fade.

She had never felt so alien before in her life. She could hold her own at a literary cocktail party, could hobnob with wealthy patrons of the arts, could blend in with rock-and-roll crowds. But when placed with a family whose sphere was limited to the daily activities of job, church, and school, Kris was soon quite lost. Becky's parents could have been speaking a foreign tongue for all that Kris understood them.

"We'll all miss Lyanne and Adam," they said. There was no doubting their sincerity or the depth of their feeling for the Cheneys. "This therapy was necessary, I suppose," Becky's mother said, her voice doubtful.

"The doctor says so."

Becky's father looked unhappy. "Bad limp," he agreed. "Shame for such an active young fella like Adam was."

Kris's temper began to simmer. Adam wasn't quite dead yet. He'd proved that to her satisfaction just the night before. But to hear Becky's parents talk, Adam was as good as bound to a wheelchair.

"He's only thirty," Kris pointed out. "He'll recover in no time at all."

Becky's mother nodded, her face sad. "Then end up going from town to town on this tour, I suppose. Won't be the best thing for them. Lyanne hates to be parted from her brother, you know. Very devoted they are."

Kris gritted her teeth. "It will be a short tour. If Adam wishes, it can be delayed until Lyanne is out of school and she can join us."

Plucked female brows rose at that. Bushy male brows drew together in consideration. "We didn't realize that you would be on the tour, Ms. Jackson."

A few days ago, Kris had had no intention of being on it either. Now she'd fight tooth and nail to stay on the assignment.

"That's what I was hired to do," Kris said. "To get Roidan Ryder to promote the movie and his books."

Becky's mother sighed. "But that was when the people in New York thought Ryder was a much older man. They probably thought he had a wife to accompany him as well. Now that they know he's a single gentleman, that Adam is Ryder . . ."

"Oh, but they don't," Kris interrupted. "And we have no intention of telling them that he is."

Becky's father frowned, glanced at the few remaining couples in front of them, and decided it was time to draw Adam back into the fold. He signaled to where his son, daughter, and Lyanne were deep in a giggly discussion off to the side, then worked his way back to the casino floor to call Adam away from the tables.

When they were led into the dining room, Becky's parents made sure that the two girls sat between Kris and Adam. Kris wished she could shock them by announcing that she fully intended to sleep with Adam, not just on the promotion tour, but that very night. But she couldn't do it— if for no other reason than that Adam would be furious with her. He'd been very careful to keep his distance from her since Lyanne had shown up on the doorstep that afternoon. It was only her imagination, of course, but Kris fancied that Lyanne was following her every gesture with great interest. If she brushed against Adam, or he against her at the buffet serving table, Kris knew she could look up and find Lyanne's honey eyes studying her. It was nearly as nerve-wracking as Becky's parents' disapproving looks.

The night went from bad to worse when they had finished eating and moved up to the Midway amusements on the mezzanine above the casino floor. Adam joined in the games with the three teenagers, entering into a competition with Becky's brother shooting at targets or throwing rings around bottles. Kris's enjoyment in their antics was ruined by the constant vigilance of Becky's parents. When Adam emerged the winner, the situation grew worse. Rather than hand over the stuffed animal he'd just won to Lyanne, he tossed it into Kris's arms instead.

Becky's parents exchanged a meaningful glance. Unfortunately for Kris's peace of mind, so did Lyanne and Becky.

twenty

ADAM AND LYANNE DROVE OFF IN SEPARATE CARS THE next morning at six-thirty, headed for the high school. School began at seven-twenty and even though it was only a week until spring break for the Las Vegas school district, Adam had insisted that Lyanne join classes immediately. His sister had looked longingly at the pool in the backyard, but hadn't argued.

For some reason she couldn't fathom, Kris had felt it necessary to get up with them, to make coffee, to offer breakfast. Fortunately for her, Lyanne had opted for cold cereal. Adam had been content with just coffee.

Left alone in the house with just the dog for company, Kris roamed from room to room. The Cheneys were both creatures with neat habits. The beds in their rooms were made, the towels in their bathrooms spread over the racks to dry. Feeling guilty, Kris returned to her own room and made the bed.

It was still too cool to be tempted by the idea of sunning herself near the pool. She tried to work out a tour itinerary based on the date of the Klakith movie's premier showing, but her mind refused to cooperate. The time was closing fast. It was now April. Adam's deadline for the twentieth Klakith book was May 31st, but Asteroid Books wanted him to finish a month early if at all possible. The movie was scheduled to open at Mann's Chinese Theatre in Hollywood the first week of June. Within two weeks it would be showing in every major city in the United States.

Kris leafed through the promotional brochures Starburst Pictures had provided. They had considered both Schwarzenegger and Stallone in the role of Dalwulf. In Kris's opinion both men were too overly muscular to play the Dealer. Adam's build was closer to Tom Selleck's, and that is how Kris pictured Dalwulf. In the end an unknown actor had been chosen. They'd had to dye his hair to duplicate Dalwulf's dark red mane. Contact lenses had supplied the golden predator eyes.

No matter how long she stared at the full-color shots from the movie, the actor didn't look a bit like Dalwulf to Kris. She doubted that the Dealer's sensitivity would come across in the film version. That was what she liked best about Adam's protagonist. While the setting on Klakith was pure Middle Earth fantasy, the characters were very contemporary. The women were individuals who understood the planet's traditions, and worked to their own advantage within the system. Most were warriors, well respected within their own communities, and thus often welcomed as wives in other kingdoms. The men were sympathetic, understanding, compassionate. They were very sure of their own masculinity and their place as equal partners in the state-arranged marriages.

Kris pushed the papers aside. She wished she were as secure in her own world. At the moment she felt very lost. She had accomplished a lot in one short week. Not only had she discovered Roidan Ryder's identity, she had manipulated the course of Dean Taggart's life, and thus, Lyanne Cheney's as well. Adam would be going on the publicity tour.

It was the job she'd been sent to do, to get him on the road. She'd been successful. So why didn't she feel successful?

She should leave. Go back to New York. Take the Wind-jammer cruise. The release of *Klakith* in movie form was still nearly two months away. Besides, until Adam finished the final book, it was impossible to go on the road. There was no need for her to stay.

But Kris couldn't think of a reason to leave either. So she fidgeted.

Adam had planned to go straight from the high school to the health club to begin his therapy. The house was hers alone.

It really *was* hers. She'd chosen it, decorated it. She felt responsible for it. So much so that she found herself sitting in the living room staring at the pale carpet and wondering if Becky's mother was right, that it would take special care to keep clean.

When Adam came home his lips were drawn in pain and his limp was worse. He shrugged off an offer of lunch, claiming he'd had something on his way back. For the first time since she'd met him, Adam took one of the pain capsules his doctor had prescribed and lay down. Within minutes he was asleep.

Kris closed the door of his room and did another tour of the house. Lyanne returned around two with an armload of books and a new girlfriend in tow. They left immediately for the other girl's home, roaring off in Lyanne's red car. Kris felt slighted. She went through the refrigerator, then the cupboards in the kitchen, and decided nothing appealed to her. With Adam resting and Lyanne gone, she had a feeling that the preparation of dinner was falling in her lap. Memories of Lyanne's simple meals, of Adam's delicious but barely touched cacciatore, only seemed to show up her own ineptitude in the kitchen.

Perhaps it was time she learned. What else was there to keep her active?

So Kris headed for a bookstore and then a supermarket. With her newly acquired Betty Crocker manual in hand, she inched her way up and down the grocery aisles. It took her much longer than it had taken Adam on their shopping trip the day before, and in the end she had just enough for a single meal. But Kris was confident that she could handle chicken cordon bleu. The cookbook made it sound easy. She had the ingredients. She had the time. Her mood was much brighter when she returned to the house and laid out her supplies.

Adam woke to the blaring sound of the smoke alarm. Lyanne's bedroom door stood open, as did Kris's. Leaning on his cane, he hobbled down the hall. A faint haze of smoke inched its way from the far end of the house. It grew denser as he reached the living room, and it was quite thick in the family room and kitchen. A quick glance showed that the smoke rose in noxious waves from something in the sink. Checking to make sure there were no other fires, he turned the alarm off and pushed open the kitchen window.

He found Kris and the Irish setter on the patio. The dog whined quietly, her muzzle resting on Kris's feet.

Kris had barely left the house before dropping down on the ground. Her knees were drawn up, her arms wrapped tightly around them. Curled in a tight ball, her face buried from his sight, Kris looked like a forlorn waif.

Adam bent, winced slightly as his knee protested, then ignored the pain. He touched her bent head. "Slick? You all right?"

She nodded without changing position. Adam thought he caught the sound of a sniffle. The setter whined in sympathy.

"Kris," he said and pried her arms loose.

Her face was streaked with tears, her eyes red with irritation from the smoke. "It looked so easy," she whimpered. "There were pictures. Instructions. Everything."

Adam pulled her close. He rubbed a soothing hand up and down her back. "I take it the mess in the sink was dinner?"

Tears spilled over. Kris buried her face against his chest and sobbed anew.

"There, there," Adam murmured. He dabbed at the corners of her eyes with his handkerchief. When that didn't stop the flow, he kissed the tears away. As if she felt left out, the dog stuck her muzzle between them and licked Kris's face as well.

Kris hiccuped, gulping at the air, clutching Adam's arms. "I . . . I . . . wanted to . . . impress you," she wailed and tried to turn away when Honey continued to offer her own damp brand of sympathy.

Adam pushed the dog back and cupped Kris's face, forcing her to meet his eyes. His thumbs rubbed in a soothing rhythm along her jaw. "Hush, love. It's all right."

"No, it isn't. It's ruined."

Her tears had slowed, though. Her breathing had calmed. Adam held her close, rocking her back and forth as if she were a child. She cuddled close, her face hidden against his broad chest once more, her arms wrapped around his waist.

His cheek pressed against the soft crown of her champagne-pale hair, Adam continued to run his hand up and down her back. Slowly he felt the tension ease from her stiffly held body.

The dog crouched at their side, watching for a chance to join in again.

"Just out of curiosity," Adam murmured, "what was it?"

Kris sighed deeply but didn't move from the shelter of his arms. "Chicken cordon bleu."

"The well-done version," Adam said.

"I'd never made it before," Kris confessed.

He dropped a kiss against her hair. "Perhaps we should stick with your specialty."

Kris surprised him by chuckling. "My specialty is picking up the tab at a restaurant."

Adam laughed and hugged her tighter. "Suppose you let me do the cooking from now on."

"Oh, but you've got so much to do now. Asteroid wants the book early and . . ."

He tilted her face up. "They'll get it when it's due, slick, not a moment sooner."

"But . . ."

"Hush," he admonished. He laid a quieting finger against her lips. Her eyes were shiny with unshed tears, her face streaked with drying, salty paths. Her lips were parted and waiting. Adam kissed them gently.

The setter gave up her vigil and went back into the smoky house.

Lyanne paused in the family room archway. The smell of something burning had been strong when she'd opened the front door, so she'd left it open and followed her nose toward the kitchen. She nearly stumbled into the tender scenario.

The Irish setter was pleased to see her. Lyanne rubbed the dog's deep red coat, happy that her pet preferred to wash faces in greeting rather than bark. Lyanne didn't want anything to interrupt her brother and their guest just yet.

She'd been ready to give up on her plans for Adam and Kris Jackson. Although he'd flirted lightly with their guest, Lyanne had begun to think the antagonism Adam felt over being forced into the public eye made him blind to Kris's attributes. Perhaps Dean had been right, she'd thought, and Adam was a confirmed bachelor. It had been during the late night gabfest with Becky that the first glimmer of hope had appeared. She'd been too busy packing for the move to realize what was happening. But Becky had seen through Adam's Machiavellian manipulation. When the situation had been spelled out by her friend, Lyanne had been disbelieving, then absolutely sure Becky was right. To prove their theory, that night the girls had snuck out of the house and driven up the mountain.

It had been dark. Midnight had come and gone, which only added to the adventure. They parked the Trooper out on the road and stole quietly onto the lodge property. Kris Jackson's BMW sat in solitary splendor in front of the main building. The cabin she used was dark, as was the first floor of the lodge. But at the upstairs window the two girls were able to see the dim glow of light in Adam's room.

"They may not be together, Lye. Maybe she's using your room," Becky suggested.

Lyanne gave a ladylike snort. "Don't be ridiculous." She pointed to the curl of smoke rising from the chimney. "See that? Adam always banks the fire downstairs before retiring. That means he built one in his room." When Becky still looked blank, Lyanne's voice dropped to an insistent tone. "He *never* does that, Beck."

"Oh!"

Lyanne hugged herself in excitement. "It means they're lovers!" she said.

Becky merely looked smug. "What did I tell you?"

But part of Lyanne doubted that midnight proof. She'd watched her brother and Kris closely since she'd arrived in Las Vegas. They hadn't exchanged any secret glances or looked longingly after each other. It always happened in books that way. Even Adam's books. But the only sign Lyanne had seen that her brother's relationship with Kris had changed for the better had been when he'd given the tall, stately blond the stuffed animal he'd won on the Circus Circus Midway.

Lyanne wondered if Kris slept with the toy cuddled close to her. If she dreamed of Adam.

Now, when Kris and Adam had finally fallen in each other's arms again, she'd almost interrupted them!

Lyanne stepped back, her footsteps hushed on the thick pile of the carpet. She hurried back to her room, the dog at her heels, and grabbed the phone.

"Becky!" she whispered loudly when her friend answered the call. "You'll never guess what's happened!"

"What do you mean?" Becky demanded. Her voice sounded disgruntled. "I only saw Dean this morning and . . ."

Lyanne was on the edge of the bed, her own news forgotten at mention of her boyfriend's name. "And what?"

"The band's got a gig!"

"Where? When?" Lyanne was breathless in anticipation.

Becky giggled, pleased to have her friend's undivided attention. "It's for the week after Easter," she said. "In Las Vegas."

twenty-one

THE FOLLOWING DAYS FELL INTO A ROUTINE. LYANNE AND Adam left the house early, she on her way to school, he for the health club. Although he complained about the necessity of going through a set series of exercises, Adam was moving easier within days. Kris noticed that he hadn't resorted to the pain pills again. She was glad he didn't. The bottle of prescription capsules was barely touched.

Kris tried a few more meals. Although Adam attempted to eat her offerings, the results tended to send Lyanne out to the nearest fast-food restaurant. It made for interesting garbage. Next to the Kentucky Fried Chicken containers rested the charred, mangled, inedible remains of Kris's cooking. So, as he'd suggested, Adam took over the preparation of meals. Kris ended up with even more time on her hands. She finished reading the rest of the Klakith epics, including the copyedited manuscript of the book in which Emling would make her first appearance.

And she took up cleaning.

The weather warmed sufficiently for Lyanne to spend her free time in the pool or stretched next to it. The first week of school ended and with the start of spring break a shower of invitations to various parties at other students' homes arrived. Lyanne was beside herself with joy. She hugged Kris and confessed that it was the first time in her life she'd ever felt popular.

The move to Las Vegas had, it seemed, been inordinately successful. Lyanne babbled constantly about different new friends. A few had come to the house, but most preferred merely to tie the phone up for hours on end.

Dean Taggart's name no longer surfaced in Lyanne's conversation.

If Adam noticed, he didn't mention it to Kris. He was too busy keeping up the intensive physical therapy, working to complete his book on time, and handling the cooking chores.

Since Kris's life had suddenly begun to revolve around the promises of various floor wax commercials, she didn't mention Lyanne's old boyfriend either. She was pleased with the girl's success in making friends. The only blight on Kris's horizon was the lack of privacy. She and Adam were never sure when Lyanne and half-a-dozen other teens would pop through the door.

It had been far too long since that single night in each other's arms. Kris lay awake most nights, wondering if just down the hall Adam, too, was restless and thinking of her. Thinking about each other was about all they could do under Lyanne's vigilant eye.

So Kris counted the days until *The Warrior Bride* would be complete, until school ended for Adam's sister, until they could go on the promotion road. She wished the time would go by faster. Her hands were no longer smooth and she'd become obsessive about the purity of the eggshell-beige carpet. She hadn't taken the suggestion Becky's mother had offered about insisting shoes be removed to avoid tracking in dirt. But it was only because Kris had taken a dislike to the woman and hated the idea of using any of her advice. Instead she invested in a carpet cleaner.

By the second week, Kris was proud of her newfound ability to shampoo a rug. She was diligently pursuing her temporary hobby when the doorbell rang.

Lyanne had disappeared early, bound for a pool party that day. Adam was late in returning from the health club. Since she hadn't made the acquaintance of any of the neighbors, Kris figured it was a salesman. She switched off the humming carpet cleaner, pushed back a lank bit of hair from her forehead, and pulled the door open.

Out on the street a taxi waited, its meter running. An elegant blond woman stood on the doorstep. Her celery-green linen suit and double strand of pearls appeared extremely formal compared to Kris's jeans and oversized red striped T-shirt.

"My God!" Belinda Jackson said. "Why didn't you tell me Halsey was bankrupt!"

Kris blinked in surprise. "Mother!" Belatedly she hugged Belinda and drew her inside. "Where did you get the idea that Halsey is bankrupt? He's doing fine."

Belinda's brows raised in suspicion. "Then why hasn't he paid you? Why are you forced to work as a domestic?" she demanded. "It's obvious to me that you were too proud to ask for my help financially and came west so that no one would know how low you'd sunk, Kristine." Belinda gave the carpet cleaner a wide berth and settled herself in one of the Queen Anne chairs. "God alone knows what happened to your trust fund. I suppose those investors gambled it away on utility stocks."

"Con Edison isn't a bad investment," Kris said. She sank into the plush cushions of the sofa.

"You sound like your father. Now please explain why you're scrubbing floors for Roidan Ryder."

"But I'm not . . . well, not really." Kris leaned forward, her expression intent. "You wouldn't believe the care this color of carpet demands, Mother. I must spend at least . . ."

Belinda held her hand up, signaling for silence. "I do know, Kristine. I also know there are services that come in and take care of this sort of thing." Her lip curled in distaste as her gaze fell on the detested carpet cleaner once more.

"I know, but . . ."

"Pack," Belinda said. "I'm taking you back to New York."

Kris stared at her mother, dumbfounded. "Don't be ridiculous, Mother. I'm twenty-seven years old. You can't just order me to go back to New York. I have a job to do and . . ."

"Pack your things, Kristine." Belinda's voice was stern. Kris hadn't heard that tone since she'd been sixteen and late returning from a date.

Belinda crossed her legs. Her lips were prim in disapproval. "I didn't believe it when Halsey told me you were lingering . . . his word, not mine . . . over this assignment," she said. "He has other clients lined up. All you were supposed to do was convince this Ryder person to make a few personal appearances. Then you were to return."

Kris was mulish. She folded her arms across her chest and leaned back, pressing deeply into the sofa cushions. "I'm not leaving."

"Don't be stubborn, darling."

"Me stubborn!"

"I don't understand this asinine determination to stay when . . ." Belinda began.

The front door opened. Kris hadn't heard the Trooper's engine. She wasn't prepared for the change in her mother's face when Adam walked in.

He stopped, disconcerted to find Kris entertaining. "I hope I'm not interrupting anything," he said, and grinned apologetically at Belinda.

Kris ground her teeth in irritation when her mother gave him a coquettish smile. Belinda held out her hand, as if she were a queen greeting a cavalier. "You must be Mr. Ryder," she cooed.

"He's Mr. Cheney," Kris growled.

"Same difference," Adam admitted, further irritating Kris.

Belinda awarded him a wider smile. "I'm Kristine's mother," she said.

"Impossible."

Kris wished he were standing closer to her so that she could kick him. Not necessarily in his good leg either.

"I hope you've come for an extended stay," Adam invited smoothly.

Belinda seemed to have forgotten the reason for her visit. "How kind of you to ask," she murmured.

"We haven't the room," Kris snarled.

Her mother had always been quick to take an attractive man up on his offer, though. "I could share with you, dear," Belinda suggested. "If Mr. Cheney doesn't mind, that is."

Mr. Cheney had the nerve to extend an indefinite invitation and insist Belinda call him Adam. Lyanne arrived a few minutes later and was introduced. She appeared quite taken with their guest. Kris had an uncontrollable urge to strangle her mother. Before she had a chance to object, Belinda had instructed the taxi man to move her things from his waiting vehicle into Kris's room. Adam paid the driver off.

While Kris scowled, the Cheneys and her mother decided the surprise visit merited eating out. Lyanne scampered off to change clothes immediately. Adam excused himself to call in reservations at the Port Tack. When Kris tried to leave the room, Belinda's beautifully manicured nails dug into her daughter's arm, holding her back.

"I totally understand your reasoning now, darling," she murmured. "Even I might be tempted to scrub floors for that man."

Kris glared. "Mother," she hissed. "It isn't like that. It's . . ."

"Yes, yes, dear. I realize you aren't sharing a room with him. There is that darling girl to consider."

"Mother . . ."

Belinda patted Kris's arm in an abstracted way. "Do go shower and change, Kristine. Your Adam has promised me lobster for dinner and you know how I adore it."

When Adam finished his call, he found Belinda alone in the living room. She had moved to the sofa and now patted the cushion next to her invitingly.

"We have something to discuss, Adam," Belinda said.

Amused by her grande dame manner, Adam did as he was instructed. Her eyes weren't as deep a blue as Kris's, he noticed. Nor was her hair an ice-blond like her daughter's. But he recognized the smooth elegance of Belinda's movements. They were an exact duplicate of Kris's carriage.

Belinda wasted no time. She pinned him with a rather penetrating glance. "What have you done to Kristine?" she demanded.

Adam blinked. "I beg your pardon?"

"That is not my daughter," Belinda claimed. She waved one hand gracefully in the direction of the bedrooms. "That is a changeling. She looks like Kris, sounds like Kris. But she is not Kris."

Adam frowned, trying to follow Belinda's train of thought. It was hopeless. "I don't understand."

"My daughter doesn't do housework," she said. "Nor does she cook . . ."

Amusement danced in his eyes. "Is that ever right."

Belinda gave him an arch look.

Adam infuriated her by chuckling softly. "Are you trying to ask what my intentions are, Mrs. Jackson?"

"And if I am?"

"I can't satisfy your curiosity."

Belinda wasn't put off. "Why not?" she pursued.

"For the simple reason that I don't know how Kris feels," Adam said. "It's too soon. It's only been a couple weeks since . . ."

"Rubbish," Belinda declared. "There is only one reason any woman suddenly takes it into her head to personally clean a house when she can afford to have it done for her."

Adam waited, one brow raised questioningly. "Which is?"

"Men are so dense," Belinda grumbled, more to herself than to him. "She's in love, of course."

A slow smile lit Adam's face, starting first in his eyes, then curving his lips. "Mrs. Jackson," he said softly, "would you like to see my financial statement?"

twenty-two

IT WAS A LOVELY FEELING. KRIS DREAMED SHE WAS IN Adam's arms again. That he was caressing her awake as he had that one morning so long ago. She'd relived those tender, delicious moments often, just before waking. But they escaped her all too soon. Left her wanting.

Just seeing him daily, exchanging secret glances behind Lyanne's back, or stolen kisses between the girl's trips in and out of the house, made the pain of longing just that much sweeter. Kris felt like a martyr for love, like some tragic literary heroine.

The lovely sensation of the dream lingered that particular morning. It was probably the result of a fairly sleepless night next to her mother. Or the numerous glasses of wine she'd had with dinner.

Belinda had savored her lobster. Adam ordered a surf-and-turf combination while Lyanne enjoyed barbecued spareribs, licking the tasty sauce from her fingers. Kris couldn't remember what she'd had. A large salad. Something . . . brown?

What she remembered most was the sight of her mother fawning over Adam Cheney.

"No, don't," she murmured sleepily at the memory.

"Don't what?" a deep voice purred in her ear. "Don't do this?"

The sensations were stronger in this dream. As if Adam were next to her after all. As if his hand had just moved along her thigh, over her hip, and up under the top of the silk pajamas she wore. Probably the fault of the wine. Kris hoped she wouldn't wake up just yet. This was much too nice. With a sigh of pure ecstasy, she snuggled into the soft welcoming folds of her pillow.

She fantasized that the buttons at her breast freed themselves, that the cool touch of silk slid away exposing her to his gaze. That he bent, brushing his lips against her warm blushing flesh.

Kris turned over. Her eyelids flickered. The erotic feel of feather-light kisses stirred her senses, and at long last, drew her from sleep.

"Good morning," Adam greeted.

Kris jolted upright. She hadn't been dreaming. He was here. In her bed!

"Adam!"

He'd already returned to his pleasant grazing, his lips sampling the various rises and falls of her anatomy. "Mmm?"

"Lyanne," Kris gasped. "My mother!"

"Gone," he said. "Shopping."

"But they could . . ."

"Come back at any time?" He chuckled and lay back on the pillows next to her. "I don't think so. Belinda's message was too precise to allow for any miscalculation."

Kris's eyes grew wider in disbelief. "Mother?"

"Promised to be back by five o'clock. At the earliest," he added with a slight emphasis on the last word.

"Mother," Kris said, her voice a definite growl now.

Adam traced a lazy path with his forefinger, beginning at Kris's collarbone and working toward where her breast peeped from the jade print top of her pajamas. "The opportunity was too tempting to resist. Maybe," he said, bending to follow the freshly charted trail with his lips, "we can make today a holiday."

Her breath was quick and shallow as Adam continued his exploration. "What kind of holiday?"

"A long drive?" he suggested. Adam's hands encircled her waist and slid downward, easing the silk trousers from her hips. "I'll even be the chauffeur," he offered.

Kris shivered in pleasure as her nightwear was slowly peeled away. "Is your knee up to it?"

His eyebrow cocked in an amused query, his lips curved.

"Driving, I mean," Kris said hastily.

"Slick, it's even up to this," he murmured and moved over her supine form.

Adam headed his Isuzu Trooper north, fighting traffic back to the expressway, then cruised even farther out, rejoining Interstate 15 as it darted toward Utah. Kris was content just to watch the desolate desert vistas speed by. They could have driven all the way back to the Dixie National Forest and Klakith Lodge. She wouldn't have cared. She was alone with Adam, and that's all that mattered at the moment.

All too soon she'd have to share him again, have to relinquish the delicious intimacy they'd shared that morning. For now he was hers and hers alone.

Adam took the turn to the Valley of Fire. Kris didn't at first understand what made one particular desert valley different from another. The Nevada landscape was one steeply rising mountain range after another, each with its own low, arid basin. The road twisted through a series of them before the setting began to metamorphose.

It wasn't that the geologic formations changed. There were still mountains, still valleys. But the color was no longer just the drab gray-white of bleached soil or the sage-green of brush. Here the desert was vibrant, rich, and red. It was indeed a valley of fire.

The sandstone formations took on twisted shapes, contorted by the patient work of wind and infrequent rain. Some piles of rock had been awarded names, such as Elephant Rock. Viewed from one angle it looked nothing like its namesake. Yet, an adjustment in perspective allowed the massive animal to emerge, its trunk dragging on the ground.

Adam slowed and turned onto a side track, toward the area the park service had designated Atlatl. Adam explained briefly that an atlatl was a primitive weapon, a stick perhaps two to three feet long shaped so that one end was a smooth handle, the other carved into a V-shaped groove that would accommodate a dart. It was swung overhand as a spear might be, but the propulsion had driven a hunter's dart a greater distance.

There were no prehistoric weapons at this particular site, though. What it offered was a panorama of petroglyphs, Indian rock drawings.

Adam parked the Trooper and took Kris's hand to stroll toward the metal staircase that ran up the rock wall. His limp was disappearing, she was glad to note. He hadn't brought his cane along. In fact, the last few days Adam had rarely used it. Kris wondered if he would have progressed to this state of well-being without the physical therapy. She doubted it. The fact that Adam was clearly profiting from the move to Las Vegas pleased her. After all, she'd been a bit underhanded, using his concern for Lyanne in luring him out of the mountains.

"Come on," Adam urged as they reached the foot of the stairs. "The view from the top is spectacular. Not only of the petroglyphs but of the valley. You first, I'll catch up with you."

Kris looked up, mentally counting the vast number of steps, concerned about their effect on Adam's recovering leg muscles. "I'm afraid of heights," she said, hoping to deter him from the climb.

"Go," Adam insisted. "I'll be with you."

"But what if I feel faint?"

"Sit down and put your head between your knees."

She wasn't going to give up. "I could fall. Break my neck."

Adam wasn't fooled. "You won't. And climbing stairs is supposed to be good for me."

Kris stared up at the numerous steps that led up to the ledge of Indian paintings far above. "A few steps, maybe," she said. "*This* is ridiculous."

But in the end, Kris was climbing.

She hadn't lied. She was afraid of heights. Her hand on the metal railing grew whiter with each step. By the second tier she was gripping it with both hands. Her breath was short when she reached the top. She was surprised to find Adam was right behind her. Although he had taken the climb at a slow rate, fear had kept Kris to a snail's pace.

A long, narrow metal platform stretched along the cliff face at the top of the staircase. It allowed visitors to walk out to see the primitive symbols painted in blacks and whites against the red-hued stone. The petroglyphs consisted of handprints, circles, squiggly lines, or childlike depictions of mountain sheep.

Adam strode along the platform seemingly unaware that

the rock face dropped away beneath him. The stairway had followed a more ancient-looking pathway of steps hewn from the stone. Very narrow, very dangerous-looking. They reminded Kris of pathways she'd read about in the Klakith chronicles.

Standing against a backdrop of primitive rock drawings with the blood-hued stone all around him, Adam looked more like Dalwulf the Dealer than ever.

Kris clung to the railing, trying to look interested in the nearest pictures. Instead she was far too conscious of the height she had climbed.

The breathless fear that tightened her throat grew when Adam turned and leaned on the rail, staring out over the basin, unconcerned about the steep drop to the desert floor.

His eyes gazed off into the distance, savoring the beauty of the view. From this height it was possible to see for miles. Miles of dry land, tufts of sage and mesquite, of wind-whipped rock. "I suggested Starburst Pictures shoot on location here for the Klakith movie," he said. "Or Monument Valley down in Arizona. Of course it didn't happen. They used some patch of California."

Kris eased her way down the metal railing to sit on the top step. She didn't let loose of the bars, though. "The contract didn't allow you any say?"

"Limited," Adam admitted. "I held out for script control."

"Did they mangle the story much in converting it to a screenplay?" Kris asked. She'd seen so many movies that had little to do with the book they supposedly portrayed. *Klakith* would disappoint her as well now that she had become enchanted with Adam's fantasy world.

He laughed. "They tried. But since I wrote the script and refused to budge on certain aspects, it won't be quite as bad as . . ."

Kris was startled at his quiet announcement. "You wrote the movie script!" she croaked. "They didn't tell me that!"

"Read your own literature, slick. It's in small print, but it's in the credits. *Based on the Klakith novels of Roidan Ryder. Adapted for the screen by . . .* "

"Roidan Ryder, huh?"

Adam flashed her a wide smile. "*Au contraire*, my love. The screenplay is by a fella named Adam Cheney."

He'd used his own name. "Oh, Adam! That's wonderful! You'll be able to use that credit to advertise your new series when Roidan . . ." Kris came to an abrupt halt.

Adam still gazed out at the scenery, apparently unaware of her slip.

"How did you know I was going to write under my own moniker from now on?" he asked. "The publishers don't know I'm Ryder. Did Lyanne tell you about the new series?"

He wasn't angry, merely curious. Kris looked down at her knees. Unfortunately that meant she was also looking at the open drop beneath the steps, and the tumble of rocks below. She gulped and quickly adjusted her view to stare out over the valley.

"Er . . . I read your correspondence," she confessed. "I wasn't prying. Well, not exactly. I was looking for evidence of where to find Roidan Ryder. And . . ."

"Come here," Adam said, his voice deep and vibrant.

Kris blinked at him. "So you can push me to my death for snooping?"

"Nothing so drastic."

Kris swallowed loudly. "Well, I think you'd better come over here," she said. She gulped once more, trying to cure the dryness in her throat. "You see, I wasn't kidding about being afraid of heights, Adam."

He was at her side immediately, but his tone was teasing rather than concerned. "That's not an Emling attitude, slick." Slowly he pried her fingers free from the railing. Kris clutched at him instead.

"I'm a failure then. Again," she moaned. "I can't do anything right for you. I can't cook. I hate cleaning. I'm nothing like Emling and she's your dream girl . . ."

Adam dissolved into helpless laughter. "Ah, slick, what would I do without you?" he said, after a few moments. He hugged her close. "Emling is not my ideal. You are."

"Me? But, Adam, I can't . . ."

"Cook? So what?"

"I tried cleaning but I hate it."

"So do I."

"I'm only good at bossing people around," Kris claimed. "I wasn't patient enough to continue as a model. I'm not patient enough to take care of a house, either. I want to be on the road, seeing different places, meeting people. Doing things." She paused, catching her breath and snuggled closer in his arms. "So you see, I can't do anything useful," Kris finished in a rush.

Adam laid his cheek against her hair. "And what makes you think I want anything different? Just because I've holed up waiting for Lyanne to grow up doesn't mean I haven't dreamed about traveling, slick."

"You're just saying that."

"Don't believe me?"

"Adam. You can't leave your sister. It would be like ripping off your right arm."

"True. But she'll be off on her own in a couple more years."

Kris leaned back, searched his face anxiously. "Are you asking me to wait for you?"

"I'm asking you to take me now," Adam said. "Marry me."

Kris stared blankly, sure that she'd heard him wrong. "But I can't do any of those housewifely things."

Adam's lips twitched in amusement. "I didn't say I was looking for a housekeeper." He dropped a light kiss on her mouth.

"You don't need a wife for . . . well, for other things. Maybe if I just moved into my own place you could visit often and . . ."

He kissed her a little more ardently. "Visiting isn't what I had in mind."

"Oh, but Adam . . ." Kris began.

He hushed her with another kiss, this one insistent and exploring. Kris's lips felt pleasantly bruised. "Are you trying to say no to my proposal?" Adam murmured, his mouth a scant breath from hers.

"No," Kris sighed. "I mean, if you really . . ."

Adam's lips strayed along her cheek.

" . . . want . . . to . . . marry . . ."

He'd reached her ear, nipped playfully at the lobe. His breath sent chills down Kris's spine.

"Yes," she whispered.

"Is that a request to continue?" he murmured. "Or an acceptance?"

Kris slid her arms around him. "Both."

Adam drew back slightly. "When?" he asked.

Lord, he was so serious. Just the intensity of the look in those golden feral eyes made her weak. He wanted to marry her! It still sounded impossible. But, oh, so lovely.

"Soon," Kris sighed, and melted against him. "Very soon."

twenty-three

IF THEY HAD WORRIED ABOUT HOW LYANNE WOULD REACT to the news that her brother was going to marry Kris Jackson, the girl's ecstatic response greatly reassured the couple.

Lyanne hugged them both and shocked Adam by announcing that they'd better move Kris into his room that night. Belinda, his sister announced, needed the closet space.

Adam, however, was too conservative to go along with that plan. Kris slept next to her mother once more.

Saturday dawned sunny and warm, making the day perfect for yet another pool party, one of the last before school resumed. Belinda claimed to be suffering from delayed jet lag and bowed out of accompanying Adam and Kris on another expedition. Lyanne had them drop her at the home of one of her new friends. She surprised them by asking to be picked up early from the party. She didn't want to miss out on any of the wedding plans, Lyanne insisted.

Kris doubted she and Adam would have a chance to do any planning on their own. Belinda had taken the occasion in hand, refusing to listen to the strong hints Adam dropped about the convenience of quick Las Vegas marriages. This was her youngest daughter's first trip down the aisle. Belinda planned to make it spectacular. After listening to an evening of her mother's and Lyanne's suggestions, Kris cornered Adam in the kitchen and asked if he wouldn't prefer eloping.

When Belinda ran down, and the time for Lyanne's party arrived, the chance to get away together was too tempting for Kris and Adam to ignore. They dropped Lyanne off, and headed across town.

Kris didn't ask if he had a specific destination in mind. She was still a bit in awe of the ring he'd given her the night before. She turned her left hand back and forth, letting the sun play among the facets of the beautiful marquise-cut diamond.

"Like it, slick?" Adam took the intersection in a rush, beating the light to cross the Strip. They passed the medieval fantasy of the Excalibur castle, then the Easter Island–styled statues in front of the Tropicana Hotel. A little farther down the road were signs for the airport and the university. Adam passed them all up, hit Boulder Highway, and turned south.

Kris admired the prisms, the lovely rainbows that danced in the heart of her ring. "I love it," she said. "But you didn't have to get it. I'm sure it was far too expensive, Adam."

He draped an arm over the sill of the open car window. "It appealed to me."

"Well, it's the last piece of jewelry you buy me," Kris insisted, still admiring her engagement present.

"Don't be so sure, slick." Adam grinned ahead into the traffic. "I kind of liked the way you looked up at the lodge that night, wearing nothing but diamonds. I'm sure we'll be able to fit a few more sparklers into your wardrobe in the future."

Kris felt a twinge of suspicion. Although she was quite sure that she loved Adam, he had yet to tell her that he felt the same. He'd asked her to marry him, had demonstrated that he wanted her. But Adam never spoke of love. And he'd only proposed *after* Belinda had come to visit.

Although numerous men had claimed to court her for her beauty, Kris had always been suspicious of them. In New York it was common knowledge that Thurman Jackson had left his daughter a half million dollars in trust. The interest alone could have supported Kris in style, but she'd always needed something more than her mother's social whirl.

First it had been modeling that had added to her fortune. When her fee on the publicity tours was combined with that figure, it had taken no time at all for Kris's net worth to rise even more. Not only in the eyes of her investment bankers, but in the attentions of suitors. There was only one thing that appalled Kris. The thought of someone pledging their devotion and name to her because she was wealthy.

Lord, it couldn't be happening. Not with Adam.

Kris twisted her hands together, all too conscious of the diamond on her hand. "Mother told you about my trust fund, didn't she," Kris accused.

Adam disconcerted her by laughing. "You don't know Belinda very well if you think that, slick. She didn't tell me anything about you. She was far more interested in how my finances stood." He glanced over at her, his liquid gold eyes brimming with amusement. "Why? Should I be mercenary enough to marry you for your money, love?"

"Some have tried," she admitted.

"Cads," Adam announced. "I may be a lot of disreputable things, but I would never act that low." He paused, staring ahead at the traffic. Despite the disorientation he'd felt the day they'd arrived in the city, Adam had adapted back to the pace fairly quickly. Although he could now weave a path through traffic without gritting his teeth, he missed the peace of the mountain. Yet he knew that the desolation at the lodge would never do for Kristine. What they needed was a compromise. Adam thought he'd found one.

"I'll keep my lust firmly centered on you, slick, rather than your money," he told Kris.

She wasn't convinced, though. "You really don't know what I'm worth?"

"To me? You're priceless."

"But Adam . . ."

He chuckled again. Dropped a comforting hand on her knee. "I discovered a phenomenon when I arranged to transfer money the other week."

"Adam . . ."

He ignored her interruption. "All these years I've lived simply. At first it was from necessity. I nearly bankrupted myself when I bought the lodge property. I used the first large royalty check I ever made to get it and whisk Lyanne into what I thought would be a better environment. We had a few tough months, but then more money arrived.

"You probably don't realize this, but I used to work in banking. Doing so gave me a loathing for dealing with my own finances. So I arranged with the local bank in Cedar City to handle everything. The royalty checks were automatically deposited. I drew what Lye and I needed for food and clothing. It seemed an astronomical sum to me at the time."

They continued out of town, passing through the small suburb of Henderson. From the signs they passed, Kris guessed that Adam planned to visit Hoover Dam.

"You're trying to tell me you hate the house at The Lakes, aren't you?" Kris said. "I thought that because you lived on a lake in the mountains that you'd miss the water. That's why I picked that particular place. We don't have to stay."

Adam nodded as if in agreement. "And we won't, slick. At least, you and I will be clearing out."

"Oh. That's right. The tour."

"I'd forgotten about that. I had something entirely different in mind. Like a honeymoon."

The Trooper sped past slower traffic as if Adam were in a hurry now. He slowed only when they reached the sleepy outskirts of Boulder City.

"What I'm trying to explain," Adam continued, "is that I had no idea of what my own net worth was. The bank handled everything. They sent me statements but I never looked at them. Didn't want to.

"As you know, there are currently eighteen Klakith books in print in hardcover, paperback, and book club editions. I make the *New York Times* best-seller list regularly. On top of that, the rights to the first story were sold to the movies. And I wrote the screenplay."

Kris took a deep breath and looked down at her glittering diamond engagement ring once more. "Are you trying to tell me you're a rich man, Adam?"

"Slick, I hope this won't change your mind about marrying me, but the truth is, I'm embarrassingly filthy rich. Since I took so little out of the account, they kept investing it for me. And even more poured in. This last year the amount nearly doubled. Do you think you can stand to have a wealthy husband?"

"It will be a strain," Kris said. "But I think I can handle it."

The corners of his eyes crinkled in amusement. "That's a load off my mind," Adam murmured. "Willing to help me spend it, are you?"

"Absolutely. What about Lyanne, though?"

"I was considering a trust fund. Tell me about the one your father set up for you," he urged.

Kris did so while they continued through the historic streets of Boulder City. They passed the tiny homes thrown together to house workers in the 1930s while Hoover Dam was being built. Passed the more elaborate homes of the current residents.

Boulder City had removed itself from the bustle of the city. Where Las Vegas reached for the sky, both in the tall hotels that dotted the Strip, and in the chances for a fortune at the gambling tables, Boulder City sat sedately among the mountains and spurned the fast pace. There was no gambling within these city limits. Instead, antique stores and artists' studios dotted the town.

Adam cruised through the quiet hamlet, sure that he'd found the perfect compromise. Life in Boulder City wasn't bargain-priced. But his days of scrimping were long past.

The road took them down a steep incline. The bright blue of Lake Mead stretched out before them, hemmed in by low-rising desert mountains. Created by water from the Colorado River backing up behind Hoover Dam, the lake lapped barren shores in both Nevada and Arizona. Speedboats, sailboats, and houseboats all bobbed on the wide blue surface.

Adam wasn't headed for the lake, though. He took a turn up into the hills. The road wound picturesquely, giving brief glimpses of the lake between precariously perched custom homes. It was a lovely route. Kris enjoyed the beauty that surrounded them. The steep rock walls, the lush desert brush that clung tenaciously to the rough ground, the twin blue vistas of sky and lake.

But the road was short. It dead-ended in a wide driveway.

Adam pulled the Trooper up to the property wall and turned off the engine.

Kris stared at the starkly modern house before them. It rose from the cliff, almost an extension of it. Two stories of granite, concrete, and glass. It faced the most astonishing panoramic view of the lake.

"You didn't tell me we were visiting anyone," she said.

"We aren't." Adam climbed out of the car. "If you like it, this place is ours," he said quietly.

Her eyes were wide reflections of the sky, were as mysterious as the deepest section of the lake. "Ours!"

Adam strolled to the wrought-iron gate, pushed it open. A garden of spring blossoms spilled color from a staggered series of boxes. Mesquite dotted the mountain above them, and hung over the patio walls.

Kris's hand firmly in his, Adam led the way around the property. A large pool and spa overlooked both lake and mountain views. From every vantage point a new and glorious vista spread out for their enjoyment.

The tour wasn't over, though. Adam produced a key and led Kris inside. She trailed him through three large bedrooms, each with an attached bath, and a giant main room, the central feature of which was the breathtaking view.

"Four acres in all," Adam said, his voice echoing in the vast empty room. "It's . . ."

"Expensive," Kris finished. She paused at the wide windows, drawn to the beauty spread out below her. "It's like a castle."

Adam came up behind her. His arms encircled Kris, drawing her back against his chest. "Our castle?"

"How much is it?"

He hedged. "My bankers tell me I've got to spend some money," he said. "They don't like my tax bracket. Do you like the house?"

Kris sighed in longing. "I'd do anything for this place," she admitted. "Even end my trust fund."

"Drastic measures, indeed," Adam murmured at her ear. "I think I can wrangle a deal without touching your nest egg."

"How much?" she asked again.

He nuzzled her neck, his lips warm and distracting. "Total? Three and a quarter."

"Just three hundred twenty-five thousand?"

"Er . . . three and a quarter *million*, actually."

Kris spun in his arms. "Adam! That's . . ."

"Reasonable," he said. "Just for the view. It's a good investment. It's close to the city without being in it. The view is . . . well, incredible, and I can still fish all I want without a long drive."

"But . . ."

"A million down, and thirty years thralldom for the balance," he said. "The white carpet has got to go, though. I don't want you spending all your time fretting about it. Your mother has very strict ideas on what she feels your wifely duties include." He grinned softly. "Needless to say, carpet cleaning isn't on the list."

"Oh, but it's still too . . ."

To stop further argument, Adam kissed her. "Of course, I've got a few ideas on those wifely duties myself," he murmured.

His voice was husky, teasing, intimate. Kris felt a shiver of delight just at the sound of it.

"Think you can limit your promotional tour abilities to pushing my stuff?" Adam asked.

Kris pulled slightly back in his arms. "You're willing to go on the road?"

"With you as the guide? As often as possible, slick. No reason why we can't have the best of both worlds, is there?"

He was surprised when she didn't appear eager. "You don't want to give up your career, do you," he said.

He sounded so hurt, so disappointed. Kris hugged Adam tight. "No. But I thought maybe that . . . well . . ." She looked away, out at the view rather than meet his eyes.

"What, love?"

"Well, I thought maybe Lyanne might like to be an aunt," Kris mumbled. "But maybe you don't want to be a father. You've been one to Lyanne for so long . . ."

Adam captured her chin, turned Kris's face up to his. "I'd love to be one," he said. "I've only been practicing so far. When do you want to start?"

It was amazing that he could look so tender and so amused at the same time. Kris felt a welling of love in her chest. "You had a key to this house," she murmured. "Does that mean it's yours already?"

His grin widened. His arms tightened. "All the papers need is your signature. Until then, they trusted me. Why?"

Kris ran her forefinger across his broadly muscled chest. It was still such a strange sensation to have him towering over her. Adam made her feel small, fragile . . . and so desirable. Kris had felt gawky with most men. Had been their equal in height. Their superior in achievement. But Adam . . . Although she felt extremely feminine around him, Adam also made her feel his equal.

"Well . . ." she cooed. "There are a number of rooms that we could christen. Starting . . . here, maybe? Now?"

twenty-four

LYANNE FELT CLAUSTROPHOBIC. TY BUTLER HAD SEEMED so nice earlier. Now he pushed her, crowded her.

He was one of the most popular hunks at school. His hair was nearly blue-black. He wore it swept back, short on the sides, and falling in long curls in back. His eyes were a lovely shade of green, and so intense. She, like many girls before her, had felt a certain pull to his enigmatic smile.

Of course, Ty was popular. He was handsome, and knew it. His parents had given him a Porsche. He had been the star player on the basketball team the past year, his senior year. He had been the overwhelming choice for homecoming king. Girls languished in his wake.

Lyanne had been pleased when Ty had singled her out. He was rather self-centered, not warm and giving like Dean. But it was good for her ego to have Ty so attentive at school.

She hadn't expected the pool party that day to be so small. Only a select number of girls and boys had been invited. Although it was held at the home of one of her new girlfriends, Lyanne soon found that Ty had controlled the guest list. Shelly Dole fancied herself in love with Ty and would do anything for him. Lyanne had already been privy to Shelly's embarrassingly detailed accounts of her dates with Ty. Yet, as intimate as Shelly and Ty had been, he rarely showed the eager girl even common courtesy.

Watching them only made Lyanne glad that she had already found the man she wanted to marry. Dean was so thoughtful, so wonderful compared to the callous boys she now met.

Lyanne had been one of the earliest arrivals that day. Shelly had taken one look at Lyanne's one-piece suit with its modest neckline and had immediately dragged the girl into her bedroom.

She dug into her dresser drawer and tossed a two-piece suit at Lyanne. "You can't hide that awesome figure," Shelly insisted. "Besides, the rest of the girls will be in bikinis. I don't want you to feel left out."

Her new friend sounded sincere. Lyanne wasn't sure if she'd feel comfortable in the tiny scraps that made up the borrowed suit. She wasn't used to displaying that much flesh. Adam might complain about her short skirts and off-the-shoulder blouses, but they did cover her. The borrowed bikini made her feel like she was in her underwear.

She changed, though, and was glad she'd brought her own beach jacket along. At least it hid the suit from view.

The bikini was made of white spandex. There were no straps. The bandeau top seemed molded to the lush curves of her breasts. Lyanne felt like it was constantly slipping, exposing even more of her chest. The bikini bottom was small, dipping low across her abdomen and barely covering her buttocks. So as not to insult Shelly, Lyanne wore the borrowed suit, but she felt embarrassed, as if everyone was staring at her.

The other guests began arriving. The boys wore brightly designed, long-legged shorts that hung low on their narrow hips. Some wore medallions that sparkled against sun-bronzed chests. The girls, as Shelly had predicted, were decked out in the smallest strips of cloth imaginable. Although Lyanne felt nearly naked, the suits of two of the other girls were even smaller.

Lyanne arranged her robe to hide her own blushing flesh and tried to look as relaxed as the other kids. As the afternoon progressed, though, she became uneasy. Shelly's parents left the party unchaperoned and soon cans of beer made their appearance. The boys challenged each other to chug-a-lug contests with the other girls urging them on. The more they drank, the more the couples tended to pair off, to disappear into the house.

This was nothing like the other pool parties she'd attended, Lyanne realized. She wished she'd driven herself over rather than had Adam and Kris drop her off. She wanted to go home. It was still too early to expect her brother to have returned to the house, though. And Belinda had mentioned her intention of doing more shopping. There was no one she could call, no way to get home. So Lyanne endured, trying to look unconcerned about the tone of the party.

The afternoon dragged on. When it was nearly time for Adam to pick her up, Lyanne had successfully eluded all attempts to get her in the pool, had refused all offers of alcoholic beverages. Had even managed not to look too shocked when one of the other girls decided to go topless.

But she had not managed to escape Ty Butler's attention.

Lyanne had watched closely for a time when most of the guests had returned to the pool. She needed to change back into her own swimsuit, to gather her clothes. Slowly she eased her way back into the house.

It was shadowed inside. The blinds had been drawn against the glare of the afternoon sun. The hall was particularly dark. The bedroom doors were all closed, cutting down further on the visibility. Lyanne inched her way to Shelly's room at the far end of the corridor.

From behind her, a strong arm encircled Lyanne's waist and pulled her back. "Oh, no, you don't," a voice murmured in her ear. A hand brushed aside her long strawberry-blond hair, lips nuzzled her neck.

Lyanne froze. "I have to leave soon," she said.

Ty Butler turned her stiff form easily. He pinned Lyanne to the wall, his hands familiarly pulling aside her cover-up, exposing the scanty suit. "Ooh, baby," he murmured in admiration. "You been holding out."

Lyanne twisted away, tried to pull her jacket closed. Ty was stronger, though. He bent toward her, pressing his groin intimately against hers. When he tried to kiss her, Lyanne turned her head away.

He smelled of beer, of sweat. Undeterred by her efforts to break free, Ty bent his lips to Lyanne's throat. One hand fondled her breast, the other slid down her back to cup her buttocks. He ground himself against her.

Lyanne panicked. The loud blare of rock music drowned out the sounds of the others in the backyard. She pushed frantically against Ty's chest, squirming to free herself.

"Yeah, that's the way, baby," he muttered, his breath fast and hard. "God, I've been wanting to get you in bed all day. You knew it, too. That's why you were just lying out there, all sprawled out on that lawn chair. Just stirring me up."

He groaned, thrusting against her. "Well, you did it, baby. Now I'm gonna—"

"Lyanne!" a voice shouted above the music. "Time to go!"

Lyanne stopped struggling. "Adam," she breathed in relief. She pushed at Ty again and raised her voice. It trembled. "Adam! Here! I'm here!"

Ty staggered back just enough for Lyanne to get free. "I'll get my things," she shouted and dashed for Shelly's room. She didn't waste time changing now. Instead, she swooped her clothes and purse up and ran back down the hall.

Robbed of his chance, Ty sauntered cockily back to the living room where Adam and Kris waited. He postured, and made no attempt to disguise the leer he gave Lyanne. She cowered behind her brother's tall form. "Too bad Lyanne's gotta leave early," he said. "I could always bring her home later."

"Thanks," Lyanne answered hurriedly and pulled open the front door. "But we've got company visiting." She nearly pulled her brother out the door.

Kris lingered a moment more. She recognized Ty's type, had seen the confusion of fear and relief in Lyanne's face. Once Adam's back was turned, Kris gave the boy a long, lingering look. "Listen, stud," she purred and moved closer to him. "Leave little girls alone, hmm? They don't know how to . . . please, if you know what I mean." Her hand snaked over his shoulder, brushed through Ty's slicked-back hair.

Adam stood quietly in the doorway. Lyanne was already huddled in the back seat of the Trooper. Although she tried to disguise the fright she'd just had, Adam hadn't been taken in. He recognized a randy male when he saw one. The kid in the electric-colored shorts had been thrusting his pelvis forward as proudly as any cock of the walk. Adam had glimpsed the scanty swimsuit that Lyanne tried to cover. He'd taken in the condescending, oily smile of the kid. Knowing his sister was safe in the car, Adam had returned to put a little scare into the boy.

But someone else had beaten him to the task.

The twist of Kris's lips was sultry. Her movements promised erotic pleasure. While Adam watched from the doorway, the boy moved in on her, his arm going around her waist to pull her close. Kris leaned into him, her lips a breath from his. Then her knee made swift contact with his groin. The young man doubled over.

"You touch Lyanne Cheney again, or even think about it, sport, and I'll make sure you get a chance to sing in the boys' choir. Permanently," Kris growled and turned on her heel.

She stopped abruptly when she saw Adam waiting for her. But the golden feral eyes were trained on the boy who now knelt on the floor nursing his injury.

"And if she doesn't," Adam promised in a dangerous rumble, "I will."

The kid glared at them, then bent over and was sick.

Adam closed the door quietly behind them. He dropped a possessive arm around Kris's shoulders. His heart swelled with tender pride. This wonderful, gorgeous creature loved him. Was going to be his wife. And the most amazing thing about her was that she snarled like a lioness when his sister was threatened. He couldn't have written a better scene for Emling. The fact that it was Kris who had done this particular battle made his life complete.

"Ms. Jackson, have I told you that I love you?" Adam asked.

Kris looked up at him, at the way his beloved features softened. A lock of dark reddish hair fell forward over his brow. The sun shone in his wolf eyes. "Not that I can recall," she said.

"Then I'll just have to devote the rest of my life to telling you so," Adam murmured.

"And showing me?"

"Frequently. What do you say to stealing away tomorrow?"

"To go back out to our castle?" she asked.

"To sneak downtown and get married," Adam said.

It was a plan apparently doomed to failure, though. When they returned to the house they found Belinda entertaining two visitors.

Lyanne took one look at them and hurled herself into Dean Taggart's arms. He cuddled her close but restrained the urge to plant kisses on her upturned face. Lyanne wasn't as timid. Dean was quite breathless when she finished. At his feet, the Irish setter beat her tail ecstatically against the carpet.

Her arms around the man she loved, Lyanne turned to her brother. "I'm going to marry Dean," she announced. "I know you think I'm too young to know what I want, but I do." She turned to Dean with a glowing smile. "His band is playing here in Vegas this week, you know."

"Only two nights," Taggart explained. "We've only got a month's contract. We've already played Bakersfield. It's Ely next. Nothing big, but long enough to find out if we're any good."

Lyanne's face beamed with pleasure. "You're wonderful," she insisted. "But don't worry, Adam. We're going to wait till I graduate from high school before we even think about getting married. I'm not going to see any other boys, though." She gave Dean a glowing look. "I know what I want."

Kris sank down on the sofa. "If that's the case, I guess I won't have to teach you how to defend yourself against creeps like that guy at the party."

"What guy?" Dean asked, bristling for battle.

Lyanne cuddled closer to him. "Nobody," she cooed, then turned back to her brother. "Is it all right, Adam? After all, Mommy married Daddy when she was just seventeen. I'll be eighteen."

Feeling a bit trapped, not only by the recitation of family history, but by the tender regard apparent in his sister's face when she looked at Dean, Adam shrugged. Kris found his hand and squeezed it. "We'll see," was all he said.

Belinda looked smugly pleased, though. "All will work out for the best," she declared. "Adam, you haven't met Joel Halsey. Adam Cheney," she introduced.

"Krissy's mentor," Halsey added, getting to his feet and offering his hand. "You did the Klakith screenplay, didn't you?"

Adam smiled and gripped Halsey's hand. Kris's boss was nothing like he'd pictured. The man was tall, spare, and dressed in obviously custom-made clothes. Of indeterminate middle age, Halsey was as dapper as David Niven in *The Pink Panther*.

Joel Halsey observed Adam just as closely. "You're Ryder's agent, right?"

Before Adam could answer, Kris leaned forward. "Yes, he is. And, you might as well know now, Halsey, Ryder refuses to go on tour."

If he was surprised at Kris's sudden desire to protect the mystery surrounding Roidan Ryder's identity, Adam didn't show it. He sat down next to her on the sofa.

"You might also know that this is Kristine's last assignment," Adam said. "She's agreed to marry me."

Kris thrust her left hand under her boss's nose so that he could be dazzled by her ring. It convinced him that what Adam said was true.

"Rather sudden, isn't it?" Halsey asked.

"But wonderful," Belinda declared.

Lyanne beamed up at Dean. "Just like I told you," she said smugly.

Halsey squinted thoughtfully at the couple. "Just because Ryder won't commit, doesn't mean we need to forget about a promotion tour," he murmured. "Do you realize you resemble Dalwulf, Cheney? And that Krissy could be a double for this new character Emling?"

Adam's eyes danced with amusement. "Now that you mention it, Kris does have a bit of Emling in her makeup."

"Would *you* be willing to go on tour?" Halsey demanded. He leaned forward. "Listen to me a moment before you refuse. Your client is an enigma. No one knows him, what his background is, what he looks like. Nothing. If he's willing, you could play him."

"Play him?" Adam echoed faintly.

"Yeah. Pretend to be Roidan Ryder. The fans will accept you. Hell, you look like the Dealer. And when the next book comes out and Emling makes her appearance, having Krissy along will just add to the excitement for them. Not only would they be meeting Ryder, they'd be meeting Dalwulf and Emling."

Adam seemed to give it some consideration. "It would be up to Ryder, of course," he said slowly, as if tempted but unable to commit.

"Oh, I'm sure Roidan will agree, Adam," Lyanne chirped, her voice nearly bubbling with suppressed laughter.

"I couldn't answer for Kris either," Adam continued, still sounding tentative.

Halsey brushed that aside. "Nonsense. Krissy's always ready to do what's needed, aren't you, baby doll?"

"I am not," Kris insisted. "I'm quitting, remember?"

Belinda wouldn't be left out of the discussion. "Being on tour with your husband won't be like working, darling," she claimed. "Besides, look at all the models who become actresses. You were a wonderful model. Now you'll just be able to try your hand at acting."

"Won't have to," Halsey said. "I've read the manuscript and know what the Emling character is like. Krissy could have posed for the woman. She won't have to act."

"But . . ."

"Nonsense, darling," Belinda said. "It's settled then. You and Adam will begin promoting the movie . . . when? Adam, dear, how is the book progressing? Almost done?"

Kris glared at her mother. "Adam's not writing *The Warrior Bride*," she hissed. "Roidan Ryder is."

Belinda waved that small detail aside. "Don't be silly, dear. Halsey, you might as well know, there is no Roidan Ryder. Adam's the author of all those books."

"*Mother!*"

Adam held his irate fiancée in her seat. "Give it up, slick. Belinda doesn't believe in secrets. The cover-up's over."

"Even better!" Halsey declared. "We can play this up and . . . when did you say the next book will be finished?"

"It will be at Asteroid Books by the end of May," Adam said, "and not a week earlier."

"And of course we've got the wedding coming up, Halsey," Belinda insisted. "They can't possibly go anywhere until after that. Or their honeymoon . . ."

Kris let the voices drone on around her. It would be impossible to get a word in anyway. As if he agreed with her, Adam tugged on her hand and drew her out to the kitchen. The sound of voices was only hushed a bit by distance.

Adam settled back against the counter, his arms around Kris. "What do you think, love? Shall we play Emling and Dalwulf for the hordes?"

"What about Lyanne? What about Dean?" She snuggled close to him. "I didn't do such a great job of separating them, did I? But considering the pack at that party this afternoon, I don't think Lyanne ever needed any taming, Adam. She's a sweet, well-behaved young woman."

He nodded. "Who's set her mind on having Dean Taggart." He sighed in resignation. "I'd be a fool to try to stop her, wouldn't I?"

"Afraid so."

"Two years is a long time," he said. "They could change their minds."

"Maybe," Kris agreed.

"But doubtful. If we waited two years, would you change your mind?"

Kris drew in her breath, afraid that he meant to delay their marriage. "No," she said quietly.

Adam's arms tightened around her. "Me neither. Unfortunately, I don't think Lye or Dean are going to change their minds either."

"What are you going to do?"

"For one thing? Keep extremely quiet about the size of Lyanne's trust fund." Adam put his forehead against Kris's. "How decent a musician is Dean?"

Kris grinned. "He's no Tasker Fane."

"Thank God," Adam said. "What if I offered him a job as manager of Klakith Lodge? Lye'll still live with us here while she finishes school, but it's not that far away. They'll see each other frequently."

Kris slid her arms around his neck. "I think that's enormously generous," she declared.

"Very big of me," he agreed, with a grin. "Now that we've settled Lyanne's future, what about ours?"

Kris laughed softly. "As if Mother would give us a chance," she said.

"But you forget my specialty, slick. I'm such a thorough guy when it comes to plots."

"Especially Machiavellian ones."

"Absolutely." His kissed her, gently.

Kris snuggled happily within the circle of Adam's arms. "Do you mean we should elude them, slip away to the justice of the peace downtown?"

Adam held her close. "At dawn," he said. "You see, my darling Emling, this is the last night I plan to sleep alone."

"Oh, Dalwulf," Kris breathed happily.